THE LAST APPRENTICE

THE SPOOK'S TALE
AND OTHER HORRORS

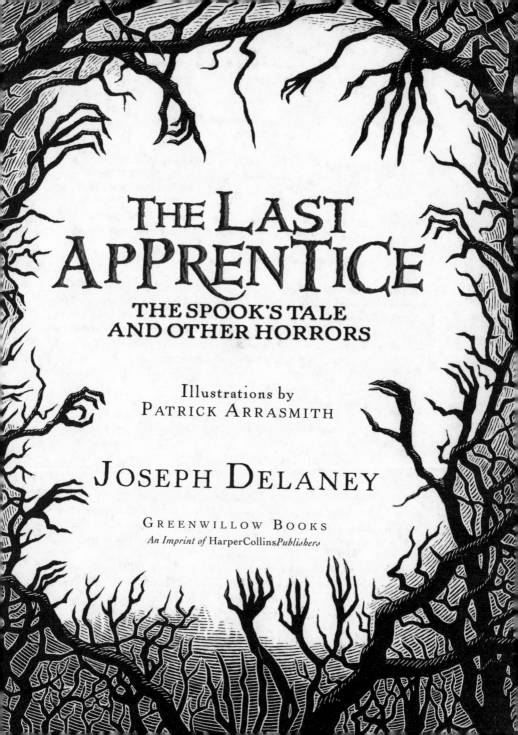

THE LAST APPRENTICE

THE SPOOK'S TALE
AND OTHER HORRORS

Illustrations by
PATRICK ARRASMITH

JOSEPH DELANEY

GREENWILLOW BOOKS
An Imprint of HarperCollinsPublishers

The Spook's Tale and Other Horrors
Copyright © 2009 by Joseph Delaney

First published in 2009 in Great Britain by The Bodley Head, an imprint of Random House Children's Books, under the title *The Spook's Tale*. First published in 2009 in the United States by Greenwillow Books.

The right of Joseph Delaney to be identified as the author of this work has been asserted by him in accordance with the Copyright, Designs and Patents Act, 1988.

Illustrations copyright © 2009 by Patrick Arrasmith

The text of this book is set in Cochin.
Book design by Chad W. Beckerman and Paul Zakris

Library of Congress Cataloging-in-Publication Data

Delaney, Joseph, (date).
The Spook's tale / by Joseph Delaney ; illustrations by Patrick Arrasmith.
p. cm. — (The last apprentice)
"Greenwillow Books."
Summary: As sixty-year-old John Gregory reflects on the past, he reveals how the world of ghosts, ghasts, witches, and boggarts was exposed to him and he later becomes the Spook, even though his first intention had been to join the priesthood.
ISBN 978-0-06-173028-3 (trade bdg.) — ISBN 978-0-06-173030-6 (lib. bdg.)
[1. Supernatural—Fiction. 2. Witches—Fiction. 3. Coming of age—Fiction.]
I. Arrasmith, Patrick, ill. II. Title.
PZ7.D373183Sp 2009   [Fic]—dc22   2008042235

09 10 11 12 13 LP/RRDH First Edition 10 9 8 7 6 5 4 3 2 1

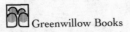 Greenwillow Books

FOR MARIE

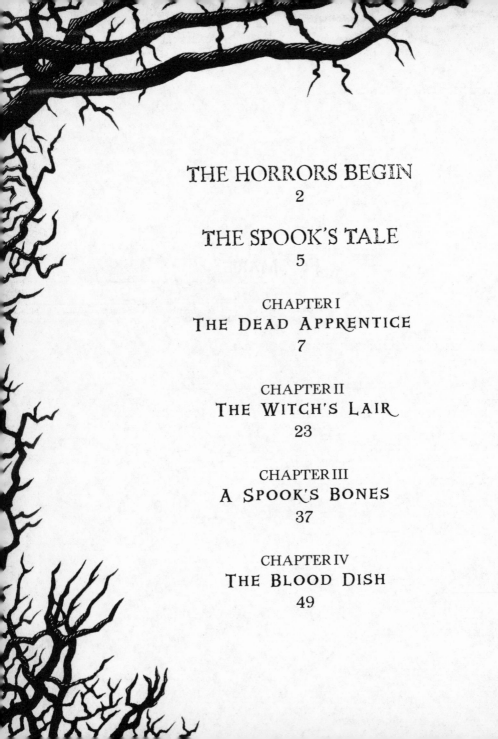

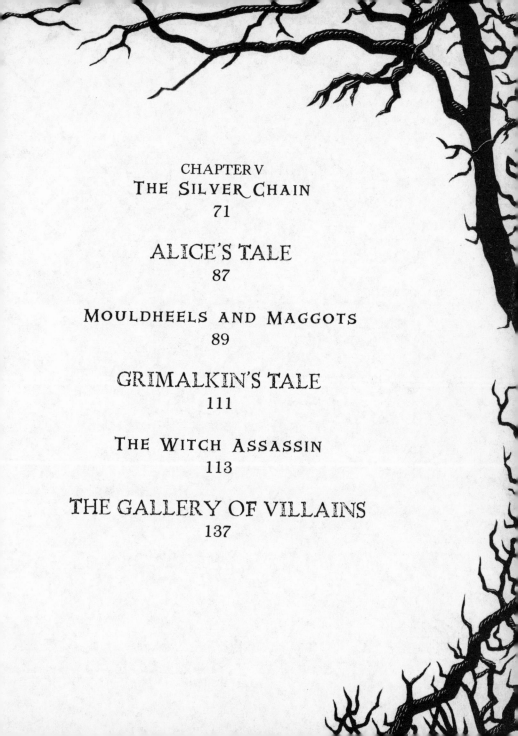

THE HORRORS BEGIN

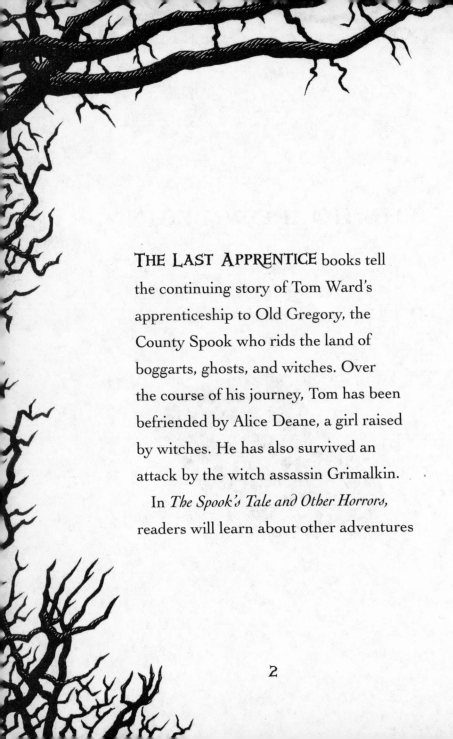

THE LAST APPRENTICE books tell
the continuing story of Tom Ward's
apprenticeship to Old Gregory, the
County Spook who rids the land of
boggarts, ghosts, and witches. Over
the course of his journey, Tom has been
befriended by Alice Deane, a girl raised
by witches. He has also survived an
attack by the witch assassin Grimalkin.

In *The Spook's Tale and Other Horrors*,
readers will learn about other adventures

2

experienced by these people in Tom's life.
Long before he was Tom Ward's master,
John Gregory had his first confrontation
with the dangers of the dark. Alice Deane
relates what happened when she
journeyed into the dangerous, witch-
infested district of Pendle in search of
Tom's kidnapped family. And Grimalkin
reveals the twisted road that the led her
to become a witch assassin.

The Spook's Tale

SOME say that John Gregory is the greatest of the County spooks. Others believe that he only prepared the way for the one who was to follow. What is certain is that from an early age, he had true courage and the ability to overcome his greatest fears.

Before becoming the Spook, John Gregory faced many terrors: a malevolent witch, a bone-snatching boggart, and a tormented ghast. "The Spook's Tale" is his own account of how he took the first steps toward becoming a spook's apprentice.

·5·

CHAPTER I
THE DEAD APPRENTICE

WHEN I was really young, perhaps no older than six or seven, I had a terrible nightmare. It began as a pleasant dream. I was sitting on a hearth rug in the small front room of our cramped row house in Horshaw. I was gazing into a coal fire, watching the sparks flicker and dance before they disappeared up the chimney. My mam was also in the room. She was knitting. I could hear the rhythmical *click-click* of her needles, and I felt really happy and safe. But then, over the noise of the knitting needles, I heard the dull thud of approaching footsteps. At first I thought they were outside, where my dad and brothers were working, but with a growing sense of unease I realized they were coming from the cellar. Who could possibly be down in our cellar? The sound of the heavy boots on stone grew louder. They were climbing the steps toward the kitchen, and I knew that, whatever it was, it was coming to get me. The air suddenly developed a distinct chill—not the cold that winter brings; this was something else.

In the nightmare I tried to call out to my mam for help, but I couldn't make a sound. I was mute and paralyzed, frozen to the spot. The boots came nearer and nearer, but my mam just carried on sitting and knitting while my terror slowly increased. The fire flickered and died in the grate and the room grew colder and darker with each ominous approaching footstep. I was terrified, panic and dread building within me by the second.

A dark shadow shaped like a man entered the room. He crossed to where I cowered by the fire, and before I had a chance to move or cry out, he picked me up and put me under his arm. Then he took me back into the kitchen and began to descend the cellar steps, each clump of his big boots taking me deeper and deeper. I *knew* that I was having a nightmare and realized I had to wake myself up before I was taken into the absolute darkness at the foot of the cellar steps.

Struggling and straining with all my might, I somehow managed to do it just in time. I awoke, panting with fear, my brow wet with sweat, trembling at the thought of what had almost happened.

But my nightmare didn't happen just once. It came to me time and time again over the course of several years. After a while I had to tell someone, so I confided in my brother Paul. I was afraid that he might laugh, that he might mock me for being so terrified of a dream. But to my surprise his eyes widened, and with a shaking voice, he revealed that he had been having *exactly* the same nightmare! At first I could scarcely believe him — but it was true! We had both been dreaming the same dream. In some ways it was a comfort, but what could this strange coincidence mean? Together we reached an important agreement.

If you were in the dream and managed to escape it, you had to wake your brother, because he might still be trapped in that nightmare, awaiting his turn to be taken down the cellar steps. Many's the night when I was sleeping peacefully, not dreaming at all, and my brother would shake me by the shoulder. I'd wake up blazing with anger, ready to thump him. But then he'd whisper in my ear, his eyes wide, his face terrified, his bottom lip trembling:

"I've just had the dream!"

I was instantly glad I hadn't thumped him—otherwise next time he might not wake me when I was having the nightmare and needed his help!

Although we told ourselves this was just a dream, there was one thing that terrified us both. We felt absolutely sure that, if we were ever taken into the dark at the foot of the cellar steps, *we would die in our sleep and be trapped in that nightmare forever!*

One night as I lay awake, I heard disturbing noises coming from the cellar. At first I thought I was in the dream, but slowly, with a shudder of fear, I realized these were waking sounds, not dreaming sounds. Someone was digging into the soft earth of the cellar floor with a shovel. I felt that strange unnatural coldness again and heard boots climbing the stone steps, just as they did in my nightmare. Covering my ears to block out the sounds was hopeless, because they didn't stop. Eventually, scared almost witless and weeping in distress, I screamed out into the darkness.

That wasn't the only time it happened, and my family's patience started to wear thin. Another night, angered by the fact that I'd woken them all up again, my dad dragged me down the cellar steps, threw me into the darkness, and nailed the door shut, leaving me alone and trapped there.

"Please, Dad! Please. Don't leave me here in the dark!" I pleaded.

"You'll stay there until you learn to stop waking us up!" he retorted. "We've all got work in the morning. Think of your brothers and your poor mam. It's about time you grew up!"

"Please, Dad! Give me another chance!" I begged, but he didn't relent.

He was a good man but also hard—that's why he put me in that dark, terrifying cellar. He didn't realize what I could see and hear: things other people couldn't, things that would make the hairs on the back of your neck stand up and your heart hammer hard enough to break out of your chest. Although I didn't know it at the time, it was a consequence of what I was. I was the seventh son and my dad had been a seventh son before me. For me, the world was a very different place. I could both see and hear the dead; sometimes I could even feel them. As I sat on the cold cellar floor, I heard things approaching me in the dark, seeking me out with cold fingers and whispers, taking forms that only I could see.

I shivered with a coldness that went right through my bones and watched as a figure emerged from the darkness, carrying something over his shoulder. He had big boots and looked like a miner. At first I thought it was a sack of coal he was carrying, but then, to my horror, I saw that it was the limp body of a woman. I watched the tears running down the man's face as he dropped the lifeless form into the shallow pit he had dug and started to cover it with earth. As he worked, the miner gasped for air, his lungs destroyed by years of breathing in the coal dust.

It was only later that a neighbor told me the whole story. The miner mistakenly believed his wife had betrayed him by seeing another man, so he'd killed the woman he truly loved. It was a sad tale, and my pity for those who'd died so long ago slowly helped me to overcome my fear.

I didn't know it then, but that was my first step toward becoming a spook. I faced my fear, and slowly it ebbed away. Confronting the dark and overcoming his fear is what every spook first needs to do.

My name is John Gregory, and I've worked at my trade for more than sixty years. I protect the County against ghosts, ghasts, witches, and boggarts. Especially witches and boggarts. If anything goes bump in the night, I deal with it.

Mine's a lonely and difficult life, and I've been close to death more times than I care to remember. Now, as I approach the end of my time on earth, I'm training Tom Ward, who'll be my last apprentice.

So here's an account of my own early days. How it began for me. How I lost one vocation and gained another. How I took the first tentative step toward becoming a spook's apprentice myself.

I left home when I was twelve. Not as an apprentice to a spook—mine was a very different vocation then. I was going to travel to the seminary at Houghton and train there for the priesthood.

It was a bright, crisp day in late October, and I was looking forward to the long walk and eagerly anticipating the beginning of my new life.

"It's a proud day for me, son," my poor old dad said, struggling for each breath. By then the coal dust had started to clog his lungs, too, and each month they became more damaged. "It's what every devout father wants—that one of his sons should have a vocation for the priesthood. I look forward to the day when you return to this house to give me your blessing."

My mam wasn't there to see me leave, as she'd already set off for work. As for my brothers, four of them had left home for good. Of those, one was already dead: He'd been drowned while working on a canal barge that plied the route between Priestown and Caster. The two still living at home had left the house long before dawn. Andrew was an apprentice locksmith. Paul had already begun working down the mine.

Before I started out on the road to Houghton, I called in at the little parish church to speak to Father Ainsworth. He'd been my teacher for as long as I could remember. His inspirational sermons and tireless work to aid the poor of the parish had made me want to follow in his footsteps. Not for me days of claustrophobic darkness toiling in the mine. I was going to be a priest and help people.

As I walked down the narrow lane that led out of Horshaw, I could see someone digging in the field that belonged to the church. At first I thought it was a gravedigger, but then I noticed he was working just outside the boundary of the churchyard—not actually in holy ground. Also, he seemed to be wearing a hood and gown, the garb of a priest.

However, I'd much more exciting things to think about, so I put it from my mind. I took a shortcut through the hedge and began to weave my way through the gravestones toward the dilapidated church. It was always in need of repair, and I could see now that there was new damage—a couple of slates missing from the roof, the result of a recent storm.

It was another of Father Ainsworth's routine tasks to raise the necessary funds for such repairs. When I entered the church, he was standing in the central aisle, counting copper coins into a small leather pouch.

"I've come to say good-bye, Father," I told him, my voice echoing from the high ceiling.

"Are you looking forward to it, John?" he asked, his eyes bright with excitement. It was almost as if he were going rather than me.

"Aye, Father. I can't wait to get started on my studies. The Latin you've taught me should help me get off to a good start."

"Well, you've been a good, diligent pupil, my boy. My hope is that one day you'll come back and take over this parish. It would be a fine thing if a member of the local flock could one day be its shepherd. That would be fitting, John. Very fitting indeed. I can't carry on forever."

Father Ainsworth was a small, wiry, gray-haired man, well into his sixties. He still looked fit and far from ready to retire, but someone would need to take over this small church one day. I remember thinking how proud that would make my dad—one of his own sons becoming the parish priest!

"It looks like last Sunday's collection plate was unusually good, Father!" I said, looking down at the pouch full of money that he was cradling in his hand.

Father Ainsworth smiled. "It was a little better than usual, that's true, but what's really made a difference is the money I got from the spook. Did you see him working by the hedge? He paid me to allow him to dig a grave there."

Although spooks dealt with witches and got rid of ghosts and boggarts, the hierarchy of the Church considered them no better than creatures of the dark themselves. As spooks weren't ordained into the priesthood, it was thought they had no right to meddle with the dark; priests were nervous of the methods they used. Some spooks had been imprisoned or even burned at the stake. However, Father Ainsworth was a tolerant man who took people as he found them.

"I thought he was a gravedigger," I explained, "but it was odd because he wasn't working in the right place."

"Well, his apprentice died last night, and because of his trade he can't be laid to rest in the holy ground of the churchyard. But the spook wants to bury him as close to consecrated ground as possible because it'll make the boy's family feel better. Why not, John? What harm can come of it?"

I took my leave of Father Ainsworth and set off north

toward Houghton, my coat buttoned against the chill wind from the west. My path took me close to the place where the Spook was still digging.

The grave was almost deep enough, and I could see the body of a young boy lying on the ground beside it. He looked no older than I was. The eyes of the corpse were wide open, and even from a distance it seemed to me that the dead face was twisted into an expression of absolute terror. There was something else really horrible, too. Where his left hand should have been, there was just a red and bloodied stump. How had he died? An accident?

I shuddered and walked on quickly, but the spook glanced in my direction. I saw that he had very bushy eyebrows and a thick head of dark hair, but the most noticeable thing about him was a very deep scar that ran the whole length of the left side of his face. I remember wondering what sort of accident had left him with such a serious disfigurement. I shuddered, wondering if a witch had done it, raking down his face with her razor-sharp talons.

❂ ❂ ❂

The late morning and afternoon passed quickly, and the sun began to sink lower in the sky. I'd no hope of reaching Houghton before nightfall and planned to spend the night in a barn or outbuilding. I had a pack of cheese sandwiches to keep my hunger at bay, so it was just a case of finding some shelter. At least it was dry, unusually for this time of year in the County, but as the sun went down, a mist began to swirl in from the west. Soon I could hardly see half a dozen paces in any direction. Somehow I wandered from the track and became completely lost.

It was getting colder, and soon it would be totally dark. I didn't fancy a night in the open but had little choice in the matter. I'd reached the edge of a wood and decided to settle down under a tree and try to sleep. It was then that I heard footsteps in the distance. I held my breath, hoping they would pass by, but they just came nearer and nearer. I wasn't happy at the prospect of meeting a stranger out here in the dark, miles from anywhere.

It could well have been a robber, someone who'd cut my throat simply to steal the coat off my back. People sometimes went missing in the County, never to be seen again. The countryside was dangerous at night—anything could be out there.

CHAPTER II
THE WITCH'S LAIR

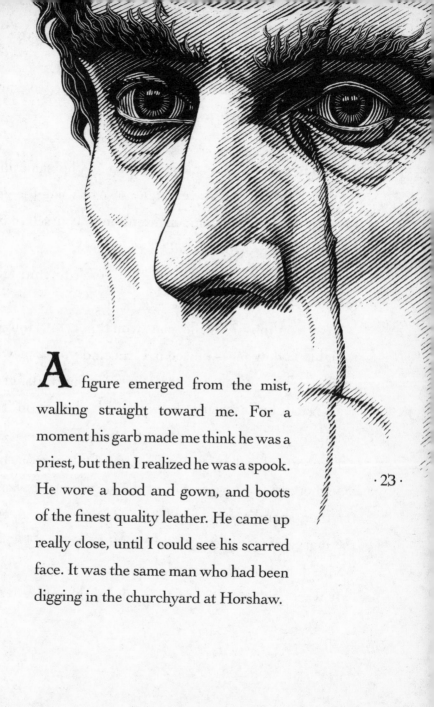

A figure emerged from the mist, walking straight toward me. For a moment his garb made me think he was a priest, but then I realized he was a spook. He wore a hood and gown, and boots of the finest quality leather. He came up really close, until I could see his scarred face. It was the same man who had been digging in the churchyard at Horshaw.

"You lost, boy?" he demanded, glaring at me from under his black bushy eyebrows.

I nodded.

"Thought so. We've been heading in the same direction for miles. You make enough noise to wake the dead! Doesn't do to draw too much attention to yourself in these parts. Where are you bound?"

"The seminary at Houghton. I'm going to study there for the priesthood."

"Are you now? Well, you won't get to Houghton tonight. Follow me — I'll see if I can find you somewhere better to bed down. This area is even more dangerous than usual, but as you're here you'd be better off in my company."

I had mixed feelings about the offer. I felt nervous being anywhere near a spook, but at the same time it was better than spending the night on my own in the open, at the mercy of any passing robber. And what did he mean, "more dangerous than usual"?

It was as if the spook had read my thoughts. "Please

yourself, boy. I'm only trying to help," he said, turning his back and beginning to walk away.

"Thanks for the offer. I'd like to travel with you," I blurted out, something deep inside having made the decision for me.

So I followed him through the trees, glancing nervously both left and right into the mist. It was said that spirits and all manner of creepy things were towed along in the wake of a spook because of his line of work. That's why people usually crossed the road to avoid passing close to one—and here I was on a dark misty night near enough to touch him!

He finally led me to an old wooden barn, and we settled ourselves down on some dry straw. There were holes in the roof and the door was missing, but it wasn't raining and there was hardly any wind, so it was comfortable enough. The spook took a lantern from his bag and lit it while I opened my pack of cheese sandwiches and offered him one.

He declined with a smile and a shake of his head.

"Thanks for the offer, boy. That's generous of you, but I'm working at present, and it's my habit to fast when facing the dark!"

"Is something from the dark nearby?" I asked nervously.

He grimaced. "That's more than likely. I buried my apprentice today. He was killed by a boggart. Do you know anything about boggarts?"

I nodded. I'd been told that boggarts were spirits; they usually made a nuisance of themselves, scaring people by breaking plates or banging on doors. But I hadn't heard of anyone being killed by one before.

"There was one that plagued the Green Bottle Tavern in Horshaw for a while," I told him. "It used to howl down the chimney and whistle through keyholes. It never hurt anybody, though, and after a few weeks it just disappeared."

"Sounds like a type we call a whistler, boy. They are mostly harmless. But there are lots of different kinds of boggarts, and some are more dangerous than others. For example, there are hall knockers, which usually just make noises. They feed on the fear they generate—that's how they get their power. But hall-knockers sometimes change without warning into stone chuckers, which can hurl large rocks and kill people. But there are even worse types of boggarts. I've been trying to deal with what we call a bone breaker. They rob fresh graves, digging up the corpses, then scraping off the flesh and devouring the marrow inside the bones."

I shuddered at the gruesome picture he'd painted, but he hadn't finished yet.

"However, the worst of them develop a taste for the living. This happens when a witch gets involved. Some witches use bone magic as the source of their dark power. What better for such a malevolent witch than to control a bone breaker and get it to bring her what she needs!"

I shivered. "Sounds horrible!" I told him.

"It's worse than that, boy. Soldiers fighting a battle rarely have to face such terrors. There I was, just two nights ago, on my way to bind a bone breaker, when the boggart struck. I heard it coming across the field, and I called out a warning to my apprentice. But it was too late. The boggart snatched the thumb bone of his left hand. Well, that's what it wanted, but it took off the whole hand at the wrist. There was little I could do. I managed to stop the bleeding by binding his upper arm tightly with strips torn from his cloak. But he soon went blue round the lips and stopped breathing. The shock of the injury must have killed him.

"That was totally unexpected," continued the spook. "The boggart would have had no idea we were in the vicinity. Someone must have directed it to us. I suspect a witch must have been involved . . ."

He fell silent and stared at the wall for a long time, as if reliving those terrible events. It gave me chance to study his face. The scar was exceedingly deep and ran from high on his forehead right down to his chin. He was lucky not to have lost the sight of his left eye. The scar cut a white swath through his eyebrow, and the two separated ridges of hair were not quite in line.

The spook glanced at me quickly. I looked away, but he knew that I'd been studying his face. "Not a pretty sight, is it, boy?" he growled. "Another boggart did that—a stone chucker. But that's another story."

"The boggart that killed your apprentice . . . is it close by?" I asked.

"It won't be far away, boy. It all happened less than a mile from here. Over yonder to the east," he said, pointing through the open doorway. "Just south of Grimshaw Wood—and that's where I'll be heading at first light. The job needs finishing."

The thought of such a dangerous boggart so close to our shelter made me really nervous, and I jumped a few times when some noise outside disturbed me. But I was so tired that I eventually fell asleep.

Soon after dawn, with a brief "Good morning" and a nod, the spook and I parted, and I continued north through the trees. The weather had changed. It was now unseasonably warm, and dark clouds were gathering overhead. I'd traveled less than a mile when I heard the first rumble of thunder. Soon forked lightning was splitting the sky with flash after jagged flash. I'd never liked thunder—it made me nervous, and I wanted to get away from the trees and the risk of being struck by lightning.

Suddenly I saw what I took to be a ruined cottage ahead. One of the windows was boarded up, another had a broken pane, and the front door hung wide on its hinges. It seemed like a good place to shelter while the storm passed. But no sooner had I stepped inside than I realized I'd made a very big mistake.

The place showed signs of recent occupation. The ashes of a fire were still smoking in the grate of the small front room, and I saw the stub of a fat candle on the window ledge. A candle made from black wax.

When I saw that, my heart began to hammer with fear. It was said that witches used such candles: They were that dark color because blood had been stirred into the molten wax. This cottage must be a witch's lair!

I held my breath and listened very carefully. The cottage was totally silent. All I could hear was the rain drumming on the roof. Should I run for it? Was it safer out there, at the mercy of the elements? Ready to flee at the slightest hint of danger, I tiptoed to the kitchen doorway and peered through. What I saw was bad. Very bad . . .

There were bones in an untidy heap in the far corner of the flagged floor: leg bones, arm bones, finger bones, and even a skull. But they weren't just animal bones left over from cooking. My whole body started trembling at what I saw.

They were human bones. And among them were thumb bones. Lots of them.

I turned around and made straight for the cottage door, but I was too late. I glimpsed something through the broken window. Someone was approaching through the trees—a woman dressed in black, her long gown trailing on the wet grass. The sky was very dark now, and at first I couldn't make out her face. But she suddenly came to a halt and the lightning flashed almost directly overhead, so I could see her clearly. How I wished I hadn't! Her expression was cruel, her eyes narrow slits, her sharp nose almost fleshless. As I watched, she tilted her head upward, and I heard her sniff loudly three times. Then she started to move more quickly toward the cottage, as if she knew I was there.

I ran back into the kitchen. Could I escape through the back door? Desperately I tried to open it. The door was locked and too sturdy to force open. There were only two places to go. Either up the stairs or down stone steps into the darkness of the cellar! It was no choice at all, so I quickly tiptoed upstairs. The witch would surely have reached the front door by now.

I crept onto the landing and saw that there were only two bedrooms. Which one should I choose? There was no time to think. I opened the door and stepped into the first one. There was no bed, just a small table and lots of rubbish on the floor: a heap of moldering rags, pieces of a broken chair, and an old pair of pointy black shoes with the soles worn right through.

I sat down on the floor and tried to keep as still as possible. I heard the witch enter the house. She crossed the front room and stepped into the kitchen. Would she come up the stairs?

Lightning flashed just outside the window, to be answered by a loud crack of thunder. The storm was now almost directly overhead. I heard the *click-click* of the witch's heels as she crossed the kitchen flags. Next the creaking of the wooden stairs. She was coming up toward me. And as she climbed, I began to feel very cold—the same sort of cold I'd experienced when my dad had locked me in the cellar and I'd come face-to-face with the dead miner.

Maybe the witch would go into the other room? This one was only a storeroom, but there might be a bed in the one next door. A bed where she'd settle down and go to sleep. I'd be able to sneak out of the house and make my escape then.

"Please, God! Please!" I prayed silently. "Make her choose the other room!"

But my prayer was in vain. My last desperate hopes were dashed as the witch came directly to the room where I was hiding. For a moment she paused outside: My heart pounded in my chest, the palms of my hands began to sweat, and the cold became more intense. Then she opened the door and looked down at me, her cruel eyes staring into mine so that I felt like a rabbit in thrall to a stoat. I tried to stand but found that I couldn't even move. It wasn't just fear. I was bound to the spot. Was she using dark magic against me?

To my horror, the witch pulled a knife from the pocket of her black gown. It had a long, sharp blade and she held it out, moving toward me purposefully. Was she going to take some of my bones? She held the knife above my head and suddenly grasped me very tightly by my hair, twisting my head backward. She was going to kill me!

CHAPTER III
A SPOOK'S BONES

"OH! I'm sorry! Really sorry!" I cried out. "I didn't mean to come into your cottage. I didn't know it was occupied. I just wanted to shelter from the storm—"

"Of course you didn't *intend* to come here, child," the witch said, her voice a cruel rasp. "I brought you here with a spider spell. I lured you into my web. And now you're in a right tangle, aren't you?"

With those words, the blade swept down toward my head. I gasped in anticipation of pain and closed my eyes, but the next second she released me, and I opened them again. She was holding a clump of my hair. She'd used the knife to cut it off.

"Without my help, you'll never get free—never leave this house," she warned. "At least not while you're still breathing. But if you're obedient, I'll let you go. So are you going to do exactly what I tell you?"

I was shaking like a leaf now and felt utterly weak and powerless. I still couldn't move, apart from my mouth, which I opened to say, "Yes."

"I can see you're going to be a sensible boy," the witch continued. "But if you get up to any tricks, I'll set Snatcher on you. And you wouldn't want to meet him. Snatch your bones, he will, and bring 'em straight back to me!"

By Snatcher I guessed she meant the boggart. The spook had been right. The bone breaker was being controlled by a witch.

"All you have to do is bring the spook to this house.

He'll be hunting me down soon enough, so I'll deal with him once and for all."

"Can't you just bring him here the way you brought me?" I asked.

The witch shook her head. "Can't use the spider spell on him. He's too old and strong and crafty. Just tell him you were going to shelter from the storm in this cottage. Then you peered through the window and saw a child here, bound with rope to hooks on the wall while a witch stirred a big cauldron over a fire. That should do the trick. He'll hope to take me by surprise, but I'll be ready for him!"

"What will you do then?" I asked nervously.

The witch's face cracked into a cruel smile. "Well, a spook's bones are the most useful of all. Especially the thumbs. No doubt I'll find something useful to do with the bits of him that are left over. Nothing ever goes to waste! But let me worry about that. You just bring him here. Once he's through the door, I'll do the rest, and you can get on your way and forget that you ever met me. What do you say?"

It was horrible. She wanted me to lure the spook to his

death. But if I didn't do as she said, I'd never leave the witch's cottage. *I'd* be the one to die.

"I'll do it," I said, feeling like a coward. But what else could I have done?

The witch gave me a wicked smile, and instantly my limbs were released from the spell and I was free to move.

"Downstairs with you!" she commanded, then followed me into the kitchen and along to the small front room. She watched me from the front doorway as I walked away.

"Don't forget, child! Snatcher would love your bones! Once he sniffs this lock of hair, he'll be able to find you anywhere! No matter how far you run, he'll follow. So do as I say, or it'll be the worse for you. Bring that spook here by nightfall, or I'll send Snatcher after you. And you'll never see the sun rise again!"

Terrified, I set off in the direction the spook had indicated the previous night, my mind spinning with all that had happened. I felt as if I'd stepped into a nightmare — one that I'd never wake up from.

The thunder was rumbling away into the distance, and

the rain was now little more than drizzle. But another storm was exploding inside my head. What if I simply turned and headed toward Houghton? Could the boggart really follow and find me anywhere I went? Or was the witch just saying that to scare me? It seemed too big a chance to take. So I kept walking toward the place where the spook should be.

What if I just told him the truth — that she'd ordered me to lure him back to the cottage? Would he be able to help me? It didn't seem likely. After all, he'd failed to protect his own apprentice against the boggart.

It didn't take me long to find the spook. Grimshaw Wood, mainly composed of bare ash, oak, and sycamore trees, lay in a narrow valley. As I approached its southern end, my feet sinking into the dank moldering autumn leaves, I could hear someone digging in the soft earth.

There, close to the roots of an ancient oak, two riggers in shirtsleeves were digging a pit. The spook was watching them with folded arms. Nearby stood a horse and cart with a large flat stone tied to the boards. As I drew nearer, the spook turned to watch me, but the men continued working, not even giving a single glance in my direction.

"What's wrong, boy? Lost again?" he demanded.

"I've found the witch," I told him. "I was going to shelter from the storm in what I thought was an abandoned cottage. But I looked through the window and saw a child tied up and a witch stirring a big cauldron. . . ."

The spook looked at me hard, his eyes locked upon mine. "A child tied up, you say? That's bad. But how do you know the woman was a witch?"

I thought quickly, remembering the feeling of cold I'd experienced as she approached the cottage. "I felt cold, really cold," I told him. "It's the same sort of feeling I get when I'm near a ghost—which is something from the dark like a witch, isn't it?"

The spook nodded but looked suspicious. "See many ghosts, do you?"

"There are two in our cellar. A miner and the wife he killed."

"What's your name, boy?"

"John Gregory."

The spook looked at me thoughtfully. "Have you any brothers, John?"

"Six," I told him. "I'm the last one to leave home."

"So you're the youngest, no doubt. What about your father? How many brothers did he have?"

"Six as well, just like me. He was the youngest, too."

"Do you know what that makes you, boy?"

I shook my head.

"It makes you a seventh son of a seventh son. You have gifts: the ability to see the dead and to deal with them if necessary, to talk to them and enable them to leave this world and go to the light. The strength to deal with witches, too, and all manner of other things that serve the dark. It's a gift. Anyway, where is this cottage?" he asked, his voice suddenly very quiet.

"Back there. Not that far north of the barn where we stayed last night."

"And you just happened to stumble upon a cottage where

a witch is holding a child captive? Are you sure you're telling me the truth, boy? You're afraid, I can see that. And who can blame you, if that's what you've really seen? But in my line of work it's useful to be able to tell when someone's telling a lie or holding something back. You rely on instincts and experience to do that. Looking at you, I'm getting that feeling now. Am I right, boy?"

I looked down. I couldn't meet his gaze any longer. I began to tremble. "There is no child!" I admitted, blurting out the truth. "The witch made me say that. She cut off a lock of my hair and said the boggart would snatch my bones if I didn't. She wants to lure you to the cottage. She said if I took you there she'd let me go. I'm sorry for lying, but I'm scared. Really scared! She said I've till nightfall to bring you back to her cottage. After that she'll send her boggart after me."

"Now we're getting somewhere," said the spook. "Were you lying about feeling cold, too?"

I shook my head. "No, that's true. I was trapped upstairs, and when she came into the cottage, I felt that strange chill."

44

"So you really are a seventh son of a seventh son?"

I nodded.

"Well, I don't tell lies, boy, under any circumstances. So I'm going to tell you the truth, unpleasant though it may be. The witch has a lock of your hair, and she can use it to weave dark spells. She could hurt you now if she wanted, make you feel seriously unwell. She can also use it to help the boggart track you down. There are mysterious lines of power under the earth—we call them ley lines, and the County is crisscrossed with them. Boggarts use them to travel quickly from place to place. That bone breaker could get to Houghton in the blinking of an eye and then snatch your bones, just as it did with my poor apprentice. And all the priests in that big seminary wouldn't be able to help you. So you are in real danger, mark my words.

"But I'll tell you something else for nothing. It would have done you no good at all to have gotten me to that cottage. She wouldn't have let you go. She'd have taken your bones, too. We're both seventh sons of seventh sons, and that's why our bones are so valuable to a witch. They make

45

the dark magic she uses more powerful. Anyway, let's see what we can do to save ourselves from such a fate."

The spook closed his eyes, deep in thought, and said nothing for several minutes. The only sound was the shovels cutting into the soft earth. I was very much aware of the passage of time. Sunset was drawing closer with every breath I took.

At last the spook looked at me and nodded as if he'd just arrived at an important decision. "We could go to the cottage together in full knowledge of what we face. There's a chance that I might take the witch by surprise and bind her, although there's the boggart to deal with as well. Not only that, but we'd be going into the witch's territory. If she's lived in that cottage for some time, it could be full of traps and dark magic spells.

"No," he went on, his jaw suddenly firming with resolve. "Let her come to us. Let her face what we've prepared. Sorry, lads!" he called out to the two men. "That pit won't do now. I'm afraid we're going to have to start all over again elsewhere . . ."

The two men rested their arms on their shovels and glared at us, their expressions a mixture of annoyance and disbelief.

"Cheer up!" called the spook. "I'll be paying you extra for your trouble. But we need to get a move on. Do you know Demdike Tower?"

"Aye," the larger of the two men replied. "Nothing but a ruin, though. Place to keep well away from after dark, Mr. Horrocks, that's for sure!"

"You'll be safe enough with me," said the spook. "And what lingers there couldn't hurt you anyway. But we need to work fast. The boggart we're out to trap will be there soon after the sun sets, so follow me as quick as you can!"

With those words he set off at a furious pace. I followed at his heels and glanced back to see that the two men were throwing their shovels onto the cart.

"Why will the boggart go to Demdike Tower?" I asked.

"You can't be that wet behind the ears! Think about it, boy. Why do *you* think it'll go there?"

Suddenly it dawned on me. "Because I'll be there."

"Aye, lad. You'll be the bait."

CHAPTER IV
THE BLOOD DISH

WE reached the tower late in the afternoon. It was a crumbling abandoned ruin, part of a larger fortification that had long since been leveled by time and the elements. Only a few half-buried stones marked the boundaries of what had once been a formidable castle. Looking up at it, I remembered what the riggers had said.

"What was that about the tower?" I asked the spook. "You said something lingers there. Is it haunted?"

"After a fashion—but only by a ghast, which is just what's left after a spirit has gone on to the light. It's the bad part of it, the baggage the soul had to leave behind to be free of this world. It's nothing to worry about as long as you don't show fear. You see, that's what ghasts feed on, just like boggarts. It makes them more powerful. But what's a ghast when we've a malevolent witch and a bone breaker to face? That's the least of our worries!"

To my surprise, the spook walked past the tower and headed for the sloping wood just beyond it, where I could hear the sound of water rushing over stones.

Soon, picking our way through the trees, we were walking downstream beside a torrent of foaming water, a small river rather than a stream, the noise growing louder with every step we took. We left the bank and descended a steep, rocky path to emerge on the edge of a large pool into which a wide waterfall dropped with considerable force.

The spook pointed at the curtain of water. "That's just about the best chance you've got, boy," he told me. "Creatures of the dark find it very difficult to cross running water. For example, witches can't ford a flowing stream or a river. The same applies to boggarts. Behind that waterfall, there's a small recess in the rock, just big enough for you to crouch inside. You should be safe enough there, so long as the water doesn't dry up." He looked up at the torrent.

"It rained hard earlier," he continued. "Let's just hope it rained sufficiently to fill those hills with enough to last until well after dark. On some days that waterfall is reduced to little more than a trickle. If that were to happen at the wrong moment . . ."

He didn't need to finish his sentence. I could already imagine the water ceasing to flow, the barrier upon which my life depended failing, and the savage bone-breaker boggart racing toward me. The image of the apprentice without his hand flashed into my mind. I tried to shut it out but kept seeing the red stump of his wrist and the look of horror on his dead face. I also turned to look at the waterfall and whispered a silent prayer.

We walked back up to meet the riggers, who were already unloading the stone from their cart. Under the spook's direction, we carried it down through the trees. It was really heavy, and it took all four of us to manage it. That done, there was a second trip to bring down the riggers' tools and other equipment, including a couple of heavy sacks. The spook then showed them where to dig a new pit. It was close to the waterfall, under the branch of a mature rowan tree.

With only a couple of hours left to get everything prepared before dark, the riggers set to work with a vengeance and finished the pit with fifteen minutes to spare. They were sweating a lot, and I suddenly realized that it wasn't just with exertion. They were nervous, but not half as afraid as I was. After all, the boggart was coming for *me*, not them.

Once the pit had been dug, the riggers went back up to their wagon, this time returning with a large barrel, which they rolled down through the trees. When opened, it proved to be half full of a disgustingly smelly, sticky mixture.

"It's just bone glue, boy," the spook told me. "Now we have to mix salt and iron into it—"

"Salt and iron?" I interrupted. "What do you use that for?"

"Salt burns a boggart; iron bleeds away its power. The trick is to mix those two substances into this glue and coat the inside of the pit with it to keep the boggart inside, not forgetting the lid. You lure the boggart into the pit, then down comes the stone lid, and it's trapped. Artificially bound, we call it."

The spook poured half a sack of iron filings into the glue and began to stir it with a big stick. While he was working, the two riggers climbed up into the tree and fastened a block and tackle to the branch. I'd seen one used at the local mill to lift heavy flour sacks. After the iron was dispersed, the spook told me to pour the half sack of salt in slowly while he gave the mixture another thorough stirring. That done, he used a brush to coat the inside of the pit with it.

"Can't afford to miss the tiniest bit, boy," he told me as he worked, "or the boggart will eventually escape!"

I looked up uneasily at the sky and the low clouds. Already the light was beginning to go. The sun couldn't be that far from the horizon by now. I hoped the spook could see what he was doing down there in the gloom of the pit and was sealing it properly.

By now the riggers had hoisted the stone. The chain from the block had a hook at the end, and this fitted through a ring in the center of that heavy stone lid so that it was suspended directly above the pit. The spook quickly coated the underside, put down the brush, took something else out of his bag, and polished it on his sleeve. It was a metal dish with three small holes in it, close to the rim.

"This is what we call a bait dish, boy. Or sometimes a blood dish. And now we need the blood. . . . There's no easy way to break this to you—I need some of your blood. We'll fill the dish with it, then lower it down into the pit.

When the boggart arrives, it'll make straight for you, hoping to get hold of your bones, but the waterfall should stop it. Denied the bones it wants, it'll sniff out your blood—which is the next best thing—then go straight down into the pit after it. While it's drinking, we'll lower the stone into position, and the job's complete. So roll up your sleeve, boy. Can't say it won't hurt, but it's got to be done."

So saying, he pulled a knife from his bag and tested the blade against his thumb. The lightest of touches produced a thin line of blood. It was sharp, all right.

"Kneel down," he commanded, "and hold your arm over the dish."

Very nervously I did as I was told, and for the second time that day someone approached me with a knife. But whereas the witch only cut off a lock of my hair, the spook made a cut to the inner part of my arm, just below the elbow. It hurt and I flinched, closing my eyes. When I opened them again, the blood was dripping into the dish.

"That should do," the spook said at last. "Raise your arm

and press the palm of your other hand hard against the cut. That'll stop the bleeding."

I did as I was told, watching him work to distract myself from the stinging of the cut. He now produced from his bag a long chain with three smaller ones at the end, each furnished with a tiny hook. Carefully he inserted each hook into the holes in the edge of the dish and lowered it into the pit. Once it was at the bottom, he relaxed the chain and gave a sort of flick, and the hooks came free without spilling even a drop of my blood. I could see that it took skill to do that—he must have practiced for a long time.

Suddenly there was a bloodcurdling scream from the direction of the tower above. I shivered and locked eyes with the spook. He nodded to signify that he'd heard it too, but the two riggers just carried on making their preparations, oblivious to the sound.

"That's the ghost I was telling you about," the spook explained. "The lord who once ruled that castle on the hill had a beautiful daughter called Miriam. She was young and foolish and fell in love with a poor forester without thinking of the consequences for them both. The boy was hunted down and killed by the savage dogs her father employed to hunt deer. When she found out, Miriam threw herself from the highest window of the tower to her death on the rocks below."

He shook his head and sighed wearily. "Her spirit was trapped in that tower, suffering over and over again the anguish of bereavement and the fear and pain of her own death. One of my very first tasks after completing my apprenticeship was to send that poor girl's spirit to the light. Other spooks had tried and failed, but I persevered and finally managed to talk some sense into her—though she left that poor tormented fragment behind. That's her ghast that you just heard cry out. As she fell, she screamed, and now the ghast relives that moment over and over again. Sometimes the sound is so strong that even ordinary folk like our two riggers hear it. That's why the ruined tower is avoided, especially after dark.

"Right, there's no time to waste!" he finished, looking at

me. "We need to get you into position before dark. Don't worry. The recess is small, but it's comfortable enough. Just don't go to sleep and fall down the waterfall!"

I didn't know whether his last remark was meant to be a joke—there was little chance of me falling asleep when a dangerous boggart was about to arrive at any moment.

The spook led me closer to the waterfall and pointed. "There's a narrow ledge just inside. Work your way along until you come to the recess. There are plenty of handholds, but be careful. It'll be slippery."

I held my breath, then stepped through the curtain of water onto the stone ledge. The water was icy cold and made me gasp, but I was through it in a second. The spook was right about the ledge being narrow; right, too, about it being slippery. So facing toward the rock face and holding on to it where I could, I began to inch slowly along to my right. I shut out all thoughts of the drop behind me and muttered a few prayers to keep me calm. Moments later, to my relief, I reached the recess in the rock. It was big enough to sit in, and when I drew my knees up to my chest, my boots were just clear of the falling water. It was cold and damp, and I hoped I wouldn't have to spend the whole night there. But anything was better than being at the mercy of the boggart.

I didn't have to wait long. It grew darker and darker, and by the end of twenty minutes it was difficult to see my hand in front of my face. Sounds became significant then. Someone coughed in the distance from the direction of the pit. Moments later, I heard the screech of an owl, followed almost immediately by the scream of the ghast. The most important noise of all was the comforting one of that screen of water falling into the pool below. But it wasn't long before I began to worry. Was the noise lessening? If so, how long before it became just a trickle and gave no protection at all?

Then I heard a faint scream in the distance. At first I thought it was the ghast again, but it grew steadily louder; added to this was what sounded like a ferocious wind gathering speed—one so powerful that it could strip the summer leaves off trees or rasp the flesh from living bones. And then the sound took on another dimension, as if a third note had been added to harmonize with the other two. This was the sort of rumbling growl that a very big and dangerous animal might make as it rushed toward its prey . . . rushed toward *me*! I realized then that this was the boggart.

Louder and louder grew the three sounds; nearer and nearer came the boggart—until suddenly it was right in front of the waterfall, the noise so loud that I wanted to put my hands over my ears. But I didn't. I kept perfectly still, too scared to even twitch an eyebrow. All I could see was a sort of red glow shining through the water, but I knew the terrible creature was there, threatening me: It sounded now as if huge teeth were being gnashed and ground together, hardly more than an arm's length away. But for that protective curtain of water it would already have snatched my bones. I would be dead like the spook's poor apprentice.

I don't know how long it waited there. The glow kept

brightening and fading and moving from side to side as if it were searching for a gap in the curtain of water. This was the scariest moment of all: I remembered the spook had told me that the inside of the pit had to be coated thoroughly because a boggart could escape through the narrowest of openings. Would it find one in the waterfall? I wondered, my heart pounding in my chest.

Its search lasted just a few minutes, though it seemed a lot longer. Then, to my relief, it was gone. Still I sat rigid, not daring to move until at last I heard the sudden whir of chains. The boggart must be in the pit, attracted by my blood in the bait dish, and the riggers were lowering the stone to trap it inside.

Finally I heard a thud and guessed that it must be the stone dropping onto the rim of the pit, hitting the ground. Then, at last, the spook called out to me.

"Right, boy, the boggart's safe and sound. Out you come!"

Weak with relief, I did as I was told, moving carefully back along the slippery ledge and ducking out through the cold waterfall again. The spook had lit a lantern and was sitting beside it on the stone lid of the boggart pit, which was now safely in position. The boggart was bound. My nightmare was over at last.

"It all went according to plan," said the spook. "Did you hear the boggart?"

"Aye, I heard it approach. I could see it, too, glowing red through the waterfall."

"That it did, boy. You're a seventh son of a seventh son, all right. It was red because it had fed earlier in the day — they take blood if they can't get their favorite bones. But when it attacked, those two riggers wouldn't have seen or heard a thing. Good job, too, or they'd have run a mile and we'd never have gotten the stone into place. I think they heard it slurping your blood down in the pit, though. One of them started to moan with fear, and the other's hands were shaking so much he could hardly manipulate the chain! Well, sit yourself down, boy. It's not over yet."

I sat down next to him on the stone. What did he mean, it wasn't over yet? I wondered. But I said nothing for a while. The riggers were still busy taking the block and tackle down from the rowan branch and collecting their tools together.

"We'll be off now, Mr. Horrocks," the taller one said, holding up a lantern and touching the rim of his cap in respect.

"You did a good job, lads, so get you gone," said the spook. "There's a witch heading this way from the northwest, so I'd take any direction but that."

With those words he counted money into the man's palm in payment for the work done, and both riggers set off up the slope as if the Devil himself were chasing them. When they'd left, the spook patted me on the shoulder. "You've been brave and sensible so far, boy. So I'm going to be honest with you again and tell you what's likely to happen. To start with, there's no way you can go to Houghton until all this is finally sorted out. You see, the witch still has that lock of your hair. . . ."

With all the danger and excitement, I'd forgotten all about the witch. Suddenly I began to feel scared again. I'd disobeyed her, and telling the spook the truth had led to her boggart being trapped in the pit. She'd want vengeance for that.

"Using it," the spook continued, "she can do you serious mischief, so we have to get it back and destroy it— otherwise you'll never be safe. And for now the best place you can be is by my side. Understand?"

I nodded nervously and peered out into the darkness beyond the circle of light cast by the lantern. "Will she come here?" I asked.

"That's what I believe, boy, but hopefully not before dawn. She'll be easier to deal with in daylight. You see, she'll come to find out what's happened to the boggart. Once she sees it's bound, the witch will try to free it. That will give me a chance to sort her out once and for all. I'll bind her with my silver chain and carry her back to my garden at Chipenden. She'll spend the rest of her life bound in a pit, and the County will be a much safer place!"

He made it sound easy, but we spent a long and uncomfortable night waiting for the witch. I didn't sleep at all, and neither did the spook. Dawn came and the morning drew on. Once it was past noon and into early afternoon, the spook began to pace up and down, looking increasingly concerned.

Finally he turned to face me. "Looks like I was wrong, boy. We're dealing with a particularly crafty witch. She must have worked out that I've bound her boggart and that I'm planning to trap her. So she won't come here. No, I'm afraid we're going to have to seek her out."

"But won't that mean going into her cottage? You said there'd be lots of dark magic traps and snares there!"

"That's true enough, boy. But what choice do we have? We might as well get it over with. Follow me!"

With those words he picked up his bag and staff and set off northwest at a rapid pace while I struggled to keep up. At first we walked in silence, but as we drew nearer to the witch's cottage, the spook slowed down and dropped back to walk beside me.

"We're not going to get there much before dark, boy, so we'll have to wait until morning to deal with her. It'll be easier and safer then. But I'm going to explain what we're up against so that you know the worst.

"The land around her cottage will no doubt be full of danger, with dark magic spells and snares ready to trap us. But inside her dwelling—well, that doesn't bear thinking about. I expect the witch will be waiting down in the cellar. That's what witches often do when at bay. They find an underground lair, a place of darkness, and defend it with every dirty trick that a lifetime of malevolence has taught them. This isn't going to be easy, boy."

As we approached the cottage through the trees, it was already getting dark. We were moving slowly and cautiously in case she'd set any snares. There was a sudden rustle from above, and I shuddered with fear as I saw a pair of large eyes staring down at us from a branch. It was an owl, and it suddenly took off, gliding away almost soundlessly through the trees toward the cottage.

"If I'm not mistaken, that was the witch's familiar," said the spook. "There was an owl about last night when you were safely positioned behind the waterfall—almost certainly the same one—so it must have been watching what we were doing then.

"A familiar can be something as small as a toad or as large as a big dog. Whatever it is, it'll be the eyes and ears of the witch. You see, a witch usually uses what we call long-sniffing to see what's about to happen, especially if danger threatens. But I'm not worried about that. Long-sniffing doesn't work on seventh sons of seventh sons. So she has to find another way. Bone magic is stronger that blood magic, but more powerful than both put together is familiar magic. And a witch strong enough to control a boggart may also have a familiar doing her bidding. Most likely it's that owl. If so, the witch will already know what's happened to her boggart. Just as she'll know now that we're very close to her cottage."

We settled down in the trees just within sight of the cottage, ready for a long vigil. The spook had told me that we had to stay alert and couldn't afford to sleep even for a moment. We'd only been there about ten minutes or so when I started to feel unwell. It was as if someone very strong had me in a bear hug and was squeezing my chest. I couldn't get my breath and started to gasp and choke.

The spook turned toward me. "You all right, boy?" he asked.

"I'm finding it hard to breathe," I told him.

"Have you ever had problems like this before?" he asked.

I shook my head. It was getting difficult to speak. But after a few moments the pain went away and I could breathe more easily. My brow was wet with sweat, but I was relieved. It felt so good just to be able to fill my lungs and not fight for air. But my relief was short-lived. Within minutes the pain came back, worse than ever. This time the constriction of my chest was so tight that I couldn't breathe at all. I lurched to my feet in panic, the world spun about me, and I felt myself falling into darkness.

CHAPTER V
THE SILVER CHAIN

THE next thing I knew, I was lying on my back looking up at the moon through the bare branches of a tree.

The spook helped me to sit up. "It's the witch," he told me. "She's using that lock of your hair to do you harm. I thought you were a goner then. You see, she's trying to force my hand. She wants me to face her now, while it's

still dark and her powers are in the ascendancy. So I don't have any choice—the next time she might kill you. You'll have to come with me; it's far too dangerous to leave you out here alone. Your best chance is still to stick close to me."

He helped me to my feet. I felt weak but stumbled after him as he made directly for the cottage. We hadn't taken more than a dozen paces when I began to feel ill again. But this time it was different. Rather than feeling breathless, my body was now so heavy and weary I could hardly take another step.

Then I began to see things beneath the trees—objects that shone white in the moonlight. Beads of sweat formed on my forehead and ran into my eyes. I was about to call out to the spook when he came to a sudden halt and motioned with his staff that I should stop too. When he turned slowly back to face me, the moonlight illuminating his face, I could see he also had sweat on his brow.

"How are you, boy? You don't look well to me. Not well at all."

"Is it the witch again?" I asked. "I feel really sluggish and heavy."

"Yes, she's the one who's making you feel like that—that's certain. She's not using your lock of hair though, because I can feel it, too. See those bones over there?" he asked, pointing with his staff.

He indicated one of the white things I'd noticed. Now I could see that it was actually a heap of small bones, those of a rabbit, long since dead. I glanced about and saw other similar mounds. Some were the bones of birds; a particularly large pile in the distance looked like the remains of a deer.

"We're right on the edge of a dark magic snare," said the spook. "It's what we call a bone yard. Anything that enters the snare's in trouble right away. Your bones start to get heavy. After a while you can't move at all and die a slow death of starvation—that's if you've not gone too far in. Later the witch comes to collect the bones she needs for her spells. She can make do with animals, but she's really waiting for a person to blunder into her yard. Right near the center, victims suffer a speedier death. Their bones become so heavy they're crushed to powder. Now we need to start walking backward, boy. Do it nice and slowly and take deep breaths—otherwise you might faint, and there's no way I'd be able to carry you out of this trap."

I did as he instructed, breathing evenly and deeply and taking slow backward steps. It was hard, and I began to sweat with the exertion. At one point I almost lost my balance and just managed to recover in time. Falling would be as bad as fainting. Gradually the heaviness of my body eased, and eventually I felt quite comfortable in my skin again.

"Now follow me. We need to skirt this trap and go the long way round," the spook told me.

As we took a roundabout route toward the witch's lair, a thought struck me. "I was lucky not to stumble into that snare yesterday when I first saw the cottage," I commented.

"Luck wasn't involved, boy. That spider spell the witch spun to lure you to her door would have guaranteed that you got there safely. It tugged you along by the safest path. Anyway, now we come to the dangerous part. I've got to go in and find where she's hiding."

We were at the edge of the trees and could now see the front of the cottage. Getting inside would be easy. The door was hanging open as if inviting us to enter, but it was utterly dark within. The spook led us forward but paused at the threshold. He placed his staff on the ground and took the lantern from his bag, lighting it at once. Next he pulled out his silver chain and coiled it around his left wrist before handing the bag to me.

"You'll have to carry that for now, boy. Bring my staff, too, and hand it to me if I need it."

"How will I know when to hand it to you?"

He gave me a withering look, then smiled grimly. "Because I'll shout for it so loud it'll blow your ears off! Look, just stay alert. As we search the cottage, stay five steps behind me. I need room to work. I'm going to try and bind the witch with my chain. That's our best hope of dealing with her quickly."

So saying, he turned, picked up the lantern with his right hand, and led the way into the witch's cottage. I followed close behind, carrying his heavy bag and staff, my knees starting to tremble. The lantern was casting strange shadows on the walls and ceiling, and I started to feel very cold. The unnatural cold that warns that something from the dark is very near.

The spook advanced slowly and cautiously through the small front room and into the kitchen. The witch could be anywhere and might attack at any moment. He glanced at the heap of bones in the corner and shook his head; then, sighing deeply, he began to climb the stairs. I followed at a distance, my legs trembling with every step. My back was now to the kitchen, and I didn't know if I was more afraid of what might lie in wait ahead of us or what might lurch out of the darkness behind. I could almost feel the witch's talons clawing at my ankles as I climbed. I glanced nervously over my shoulder, but the kitchen was empty. We checked each bedroom in turn. Again, nothing. We would have to go down to the cellar. The prospect of that scared me more than anything. I hated cellars. It brought back memories of my recurring nightmare. That, and the time my dad had thrown me into the cellar at home and nailed the door shut.

We went down to the kitchen again, and the spook strode purposefully toward the cellar steps. I let him go down five before I began my own slow descent. There was a bend in the stair; beyond it, the steps continued down at right angles. When he reached that bend, the spook held the lantern high. I was facing his left-hand side, and from the expression on his face and the way his whole body suddenly straightened, I knew that he could see the witch waiting below.

I was right! He uncoiled the silver chain with one flick of his wrist and prepared to cast it downward. But no sooner had he done so than the ground seemed to move beneath my feet. That was impossible. How could solid stone steps do that? But whatever I felt, farther down the effect must have been much stronger. Before he could cast the chain, the spook tottered, lost his balance, then fell headlong and was lost to view.

Instantly I was plunged into darkness. The spook, chain,

and lantern were down in the cellar. He was at the mercy of the witch. My heart hammering, I turned to flee. I could do nothing against a witch. How could I help him? I had to get away or she'd take my bones, too.

But then something stopped me. What it was or why I changed my mind, I can't explain to this day. Maybe it was self-preservation, because if I abandoned the spook, the witch would still have a lock of my hair. Later, she could release the boggart and send it after me. Or perhaps it was something inside me — the courage that a spook needs in order to face the dark and do his dangerous job.

Whatever it was, I edged cautiously down the steps and, hardly able to believe what I was doing, my heart pounding in my chest, peered around the corner. Rather than looking down into absolute darkness, I could see almost everything in the cellar. The lantern was lying on its side but hadn't gone out. The spook was on all fours, head hanging, forehead almost touching the floor. The witch was crouching over him with a knife in her hand. In just moments she'd take his life. But so intent was she upon her evil business that she didn't look up and see me on the steps. No doubt she'd expected me to be long gone.

The spook looked up at the witch and gave a groan of fear. "No! No! Not like this!" he pleaded. "Please, God, don't let it end like this!"

Without thinking, I put down the bag, lifted the spook's staff, and ran down the steps, straight toward the witch. At the very last moment she looked up at me, but she was too late. I swung the staff and hit her hard on the forehead. She fell backward with a cry, the knife flying out of her hand, though she was up on her knees again almost at once, face twisted with fury. And for the second time I felt the solid ground move beneath my feet, this time with a violent lurch that brought me down hard onto the cellar floor, jolting the staff from my grasp.

I was flat on my back and started to sit up, but within seconds the witch was on me, both hands around my throat, trying to choke the life from me. Her face was close to my own, her eyes wild, her open mouth showing sharp teeth. Her foul breath made me heave. It stank like a cat's or a dog's, of stale meat with a sweet hint of blood.

I glanced to my right and saw the spook struggle shakily to his feet and stagger against the cellar wall. He was in no fit state to help me. If I didn't do something, I'd be dead in moments!

I gripped the witch by the shoulders and tried to throw her off me, but she was squeezing my throat so hard I couldn't breathe. I could feel myself weakening, my sight darkening, and I desperately reached out with both hands, trying to find the spook's staff. It wasn't there. But then my left hand closed over something else. The silver chain!

I gripped it and swung it across. It caught her head a glancing blow and she screamed, withdrew her hands from my throat, and pressed them to her face. I whipped the chain back in the opposite direction, this time catching her on the chin. She stood up, then staggered and dropped to her knees. I felt a hand on my shoulder and looked up to see the spook standing over me, breathing hard.

"Here, boy. You've done well. Now give me the chain."

I handed it to him, and after quickly coiling it about his

wrist, he sent it soaring aloft with a crack, and it dropped over the witch and coiled about her tightly. She rolled over and over, her eyes bulging from their sockets, the chain tight against her teeth and binding her arms to her side.

"She's bound good and proper now," the spook said, smiling grimly. "I owe you a big thanks, boy."

With the witch safely bound, we searched the cottage, and the spook made a fire outside and burned the things he found: powders, herbs, and a book of dark magic that he called a grimoire. Eventually he found my lock of hair in a leather pouch that the witch wore on a chain around her neck. He burned that, too. At last I was safe, and I began to feel a lot better.

We sat by the fire for a while, both of us locked into our own thoughts, until a question came into my mind and I broke the silence.

"What was it on the steps that made you fall?" I asked. "I felt the ground tremble beneath my feet. Later, in the cellar, it gave another lurch and I fell, too."

"One of the snares she'd set to defend herself, boy," the spook said, throwing another handful of the witch's possessions into the flickering flames of the bonfire. "It's called slither, a spell that causes the victim to feel unsteady on his feet, lose his balance, slide, and fall. It nearly did for me, all right. Even if you anticipate it, little can be done. As I said, I owe you a big thanks, and I'd like to make you an offer. How would you like to train as a spook? As it happens, I'm looking for an apprentice to replace the one I've just lost. Would you be interested? I need a brave lad for my line of work."

"Thanks for the offer, but I'm going to be a priest," I told him. "It's something I've wanted to do for a long time."

"It's your choice, boy. I won't say anything against the priesthood, because some of them are good men who mean well—"

"Father Ainsworth works hard to help the poor," I interrupted. "He's spent his whole life helping people. I want to be like him."

"Well, good luck to you then, young John. But if you

ever change your mind, you can find my house near Chipenden village, west of the Long Ridge. Just ask any of the locals. My name's Henry Horrocks. They'll point you in the right direction."

With that we parted. Carrying the witch over his shoulder, the spook set off toward Chipenden, where he'd bind her in a pit. I watched him walk away and supposed that would be the last I'd ever see of him.

I continued my journey to Houghton and began to train for the priesthood. I did become a priest, but not for long—though that's another story. But as a young man of twenty, I eventually went to Chipenden and asked Henry Horrocks if he would train me as a spook.

He took awhile to make up his mind. Could you blame him? After all, it had taken me a long time to change mine! I was far older than the boys he usually trained. But he remembered what I'd done back in that dark cottage when we'd faced the dangerous witch. That finally decided him.

I became his apprentice. His last one. Finally, after his death, I inherited his house at Chipenden and began working as a spook from there. Now, after all these years, I'm training Tom Ward. He'll be *my* last apprentice. The house will belong to him, and he'll be the new spook. Our work will go on. Someone has to fight the dark.

John Gregory

Alice's Tale

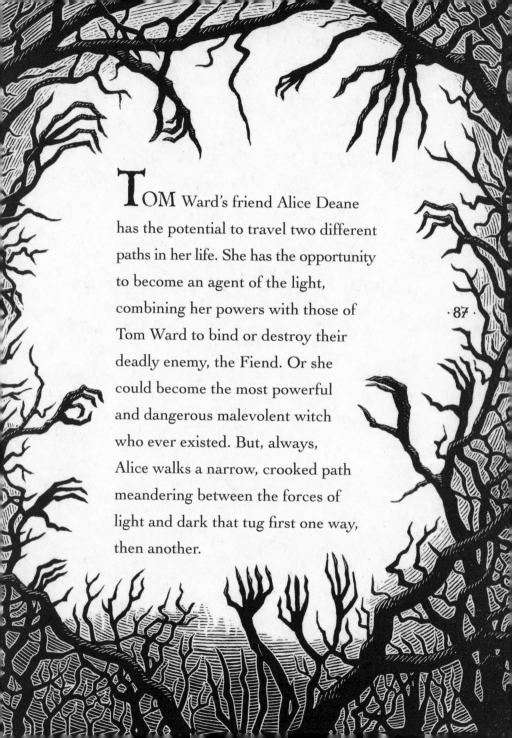

Tom Ward's friend Alice Deane has the potential to travel two different paths in her life. She has the opportunity to become an agent of the light, combining her powers with those of Tom Ward to bind or destroy their deadly enemy, the Fiend. Or she could become the most powerful and dangerous malevolent witch who ever existed. But, always, Alice walks a narrow, crooked path meandering between the forces of light and dark that tug first one way, then another.

MOULDHEELS AND MAGGOTS

BORN into the Pendle witch clans, I was—my mother a Malkin, my father a Deane. But though I was raised there, the last place in the world I'd ever want to visit is Pendle. The clans fight one another, and I've a lot of enemies there, mostly Mouldheels. Lots of spite, there is. Lots of hatred. Vendettas that've lasted centuries.

Fall into the hands of enemies there, and they'll take your bones and drink your blood. Even so, I went back. I went back alone. I did it for Tom Ward. Did it all for him.

Because Tom's the only person in this whole world I really care about—he's my best friend. Ain't like me, Tom. He belongs to the light, and he's apprenticed to a spook named John Gregory.

We'd traveled from Chipenden to visit the farm where Tom was born and grew up. He wanted to see inside the boxes that his mam had left him. Must say I wanted to see inside them, too. Curious, I was. Very curious and just dying to know all their secrets. But when we got there, the boxes were gone. Stolen. The barn had been burned to the ground, the farmhouse ransacked, and Tom's family kidnapped. Didn't take me long to sniff out that witches had done it. That they'd taken Tom's brother Jack, his wife, Ellie, and their little child, Mary. The trail led toward Pendle, and Tom was desperate to set off after them then and there. But I talked him out of it.

I mean, how long would a spook's apprentice survive

alone in the shadow of that brooding hill? Seventh son of a seventh son, he is. Love his bones, they would. Cut 'em out just before dawn. Ain't any bones better than Tom's, that's for sure.

So I traveled on alone while Tom went back to Chipenden to tell the Spook what had happened. Went east to Pendle. Told you I'd enemies there—and that's true—but I got friends, too, though precious few. And the best friend I got in that hag-ridden place is my aunt, Agnes Sowerbutts. Got a soft spot for Agnes, I have. She'd have brought me up but for Bony Lizzie.

I remember the night that Lizzie came for me. I like to think I was upset, but I don't remember crying. My mam and dad had been cold and dead in the earth for three days, and I still hadn't managed to shed a single tear. Wasn't for want of trying. I tried to remember the good times, I really did. And there were a few, even though they fought like cat and dog and clouted me even harder than they hit each other. I mean, you should be upset, shouldn't you?

It's your own mam and dad, and they've just died, so you should be able to squeeze out one tear at least.

There was a bad storm that night, forks of lightning sizzling across the sky and crashes of thunder shaking the walls of the cottage and rattling the pots and pans. But that was nowt compared to what Lizzie did. There was a hammering at the door fit to wake the rotting dead, and when Agnes drew back the bolt, Bony Lizzie strode into the room, her black hair matted with rain, water streaming from her cape onto the stone flags. Agnes was scared, but she stood her ground, placing herself between me and Lizzie.

"Leave the girl alone!" Agnes said calmly, trying to be brave. "Her home is with me now. She'll be well looked after, don't you worry."

Lizzie's first response was a sneer. They say there's a family resemblance. That I'm the spitting image of her. But I could never have twisted my face the way she did that night. It was enough to turn the milk sour or send the cat shrieking up the chimney as if the Devil himself was reaching for its tail.

"The girl belongs to me, Sowerbutts," Lizzie said, her voice cold and quiet, filled with malice. "We share the same dark blood. I can teach her what she has to know. I'm the one she needs."

"Alice needn't be a witch like you!" Agnes retorted. "Her mam and dad weren't witches, so why should she follow your dark path? Leave her be. Leave the girl with me and get about your business."

"She's the blood of a witch inside her and that's enough!" Lizzie hissed angrily. "You're just an outsider and not fit to raise the girl."

It wasn't true. Agnes was a Deane, all right, but she'd married a good man from Whalley. An ironmonger. When he died, she'd returned to where the Deane witch clan made its home.

"I'm her aunt, and I'll be a mother to her now," Agnes retorted. She still spoke bravely, but her face was white and I could see her plump chin wobbling, her hands fluttering and trembling with fear.

Next thing, Lizzie stamped her left foot. It was as easy as

that. In the twinkling of an eye, the fire died in the grate, the candles flickered and went out, and the whole room became instantly dark, cold, and terrifying. I heard Agnes scream with fear, and then I was screaming myself and desperate to get out. I would have run through the door, jumped through a window, or even scrabbled my way up the chimney. I'd have done anything, just to escape.

I did get out, but with Lizzie at my side. She just seized me by the wrist and dragged me into the night. It was no use trying to resist. She was too strong and she held me tight, her nails digging into my skin. I belonged to her now, and there was no way she was ever going to let me go. And that night she began my training as a witch. It was the start of all my troubles.

I'd only seen Agnes once since that awful night, but I knew I'd be welcome at her house now as I returned to Pendle. In fact, no sooner had I walked down through the darkness of the trees than her door opened wide and she stood there, her smile brighter than the beeswax candles that illuminated her rooms. Uses a mirror for scrying, Agnes does, and she'd seen me coming.

"Come in, Alice girl, and warm your bones!" she called out in her gruff but kindly voice. "It's good to see you again. Just sit yourself down by the fire and I'll boil you up some tasty broth."

While Agnes busied herself, I sat in her rocking chair facing the warm fire, my eyes drawn upward to the rows of shelves that I remembered so well. She was a healer, and the shelves were full of pots and jars. There were also leather pouches tied with string containing the blends of herbs and potions she used to practice her craft.

Soon I was sipping delicious hot broth while my aunt seated herself on a stool by the fire. It was a long time before she spoke. "What brings you to Pendle again, girl?" she asked cautiously. "Is Lizzie nearby?"

I shook my head. "No, Agnes. Ain't you heard? No need to worry yourself about Lizzie. Trapped in a pit in Old Gregory's garden at Chipenden, she is. Stay there till she rots! Best place for her."

So I explained how I'd befriended Tom Ward and was now staying at the Spook's Chipenden house, helping to make copies of the precious books in his library. I told her about the theft of Tom's boxes and the kidnapping of his family—Jack, Ellie, and their young child.

"Thought you might like to help me, aunt. I've no clue where they've been taken and I don't know where else to turn. Thought you might scry 'em for me with your special mirror."

Without a word, Agnes went and fetched her scrying mirror from the cupboard. It was small but set in a brass frame with a heavy base. Then she blew out all her candles but one, which she set just to the left of it. Soon she was muttering incantations under her breath, and the glass flickered to brightness. She was searching for Tom's family. Images began to form. . . . .

I glimpsed a dark stone wall. Curved, it was. We were looking up at it. Not much doubt, was there? We were looking at Malkin Tower. Agnes was using the surface of the moat to see it. Water's as good as a mirror if you're skilled like Agnes. Quickly a new image flashed across the mirror: the arched ceiling of a dark, dank dungeon with dripping water. Then a weary pain-racked face filled the glass, eyes closed. It was Ellie!

Her hands reached toward us, and I realized that we were peering up at her from a bowl of water. The image distorted and fragmented. She was dabbing water onto her face. Then the mirror darkened, and Agnes gave a sigh and turned toward me.

"Was that Ellie, girl?"

I nodded.

"Just used the mirror to be sure," Agnes said. "But I suspected the Malkins from the start. You've no chance of getting them out of that tower alive. Best get yourself away from Pendle, girl. It's more dangerous than it's ever been. Go while you're still able to breathe!"

I spent the rest of the night with Agnes. We chatted about old times, and she told me what had been happening more recently. How the Mouldheels were growing in strength and had a new coven leader, a girl witch called

Mab. Apparently this Mab could peer into the future so well that, to counteract her power, the Malkins and Deanes had called a truce and created an evil creature called Tibb using dark magic. Tibb was a seer and could also see things at a distance. Agnes reckoned that was how they'd found Tom's boxes.

I spent the night in Agnes's back room, and at dawn I headed for Malkin Tower. Knew I couldn't do much on my own, but I thought I might as well just sniff around a bit before pushing on to the church at Downham, where I'd meet up with Tom and Old Gregory. Might find out something useful. It was worth a try. But then, as I circled through Crow Wood, skirting Bareleigh to the north, the sun dappling the tree trunks, I saw a girl ahead, sitting on a stump. Staring at me, she was. Sniffed her out right away and knew she was a witch.

As I got nearer, her feet told me more. Barefooted, so she had to be a Mouldheel. Last of the three main clans to settle in Pendle, they were. Before that they were nomads. Called "stink feet" by some and, later, "moldy heels."

She didn't look much older than me and was certainly no bigger. So why should I run? I kept walking toward her, ready to fight if necessary. She had pale hair that hung down beyond her shoulders, and green eyes. Her clothes were in tatters, too. No pride in their appearance, the Mouldheels. She was one of them, all right.

I halted about five paces away and tried to stare her out, but she wouldn't look away. "Shouldn't have come here, Alice Deane," she warned, a faint smile on her face. "You'll never leave Pendle alive."

How did she know who I was? I gave her a dirty look and spat at her feet. "Haven't met before, have we? Know that for sure 'cause I'd have remembered your ugly face!"

"Scried you in a mirror. Knew who you were the moment you crossed into Pendle. Don't you know who I am?"

"Don't really care who you are, girl," I told her. "You're nothing! You're nothing to me!"

"Well, you should care who I am 'cause you'll have good cause to remember me. My name's Mab. Mab Mouldheel."

It was the girl Agnes had told me about, the new leader

99

of the Mouldheels. I wasn't impressed, I can tell you, so there wasn't much point in wasting words. Mab was supposed to be a seer. Good at seeing the future. But she didn't see what hit her.

I went straight for Mab, gave her a good slapping in the face, and grabbed a handful of her hair. She fell sideways off the log, and we rolled over and over. Couple of seconds and I knew I was stronger than she was. I was just getting the better of her when there were shouts in the distance. More Mouldheels! Lots of 'em!

Struggled to get away then, I did, but Mab hung on to my clothes and hair. Almost tore myself free, but she held me fast. Then rapid footsteps. Somebody running hard toward us. Next something hit me really hard on the side of the head, and everything went dark.

I woke up with a thumping headache to find myself sitting in a meadow, my back against a drystone wall. My hands were free, but my legs were chained together. I wasn't in Crow Wood any longer. Cottages in the near distance looked like Bareleigh, the Mouldheel village. The sun was high in the sky. Had to be almost noon.

"She's awake!" someone called out, and I turned my head to see three girls walking barefoot toward me through the long grass. One of them was Mab; the other two looked like twins. They had thin faces with hooked noses and narrow, mean mouths.

The three girls sat down in the grass opposite me, Mab in the middle. "Meet my twin sisters, Alice Deane," Mab called out. "This is Jennet and this is Beth. Both younger than me but older than you."

I looked at Jennet. She was eating something from the palm of her left hand. White, soft, squishy, wriggling things that didn't like sunlight. They were maggots!

"Want one o' these?" Jennet asked, holding out her hand toward the other two girls.

Mab declined with a curt shake of her head, but Beth popped a couple into her mouth and began to chew. "Good, these," she said with a crooked smile.

"Should be!" Jennet mumbled, stuffing her own mouth

full of writing maggots. "Got 'em from a dead cat. Black one, it was, too. Black-cat maggots are always the tastiest."

"Well, sisters," Mab said, squinting straight into my face. "What should we do with this ugly Deane? Roast her over hot coals, or tie her to a tree and let the crows peck out her eyes?"

"Best we cover her with leeches," said Beth. "Once they're plump and squishy with blood we can eat 'em! Nothing quite so juicy as a bloated leech."

"Prefer sheep ticks," Jennet said. "But they're hard work collecting."

"Ain't a Deane any longer," I interrupted, directing my words at Mab. "Finished with my family, I have. Could be on your side if you'd have me. Sick of the Deanes. Sick of the Malkins, too."

"Who you trying to fool?" Mab sneered. "Wasn't born yesterday, was I? You'd better talk now and tell us why you're here. What brings you back to Pendle?"

"Supposed to be a seer, ain't you?" I laughed. "Wouldn't have to ask questions if you knew your craft!"

Shouldn't have laughed like that. Mab was livid. Tried to fight 'em off, but my legs were bound and it was three against one. The twins held me down while Mab pulled out a blade and cut off a lock of my hair. I began to tremble then. Knew I was in her power now, all right. Using dark magic, they could hurt me real bad. They took me back to the row of cottages where Mab and her sisters lived. Got me down into a cellar and started to work on me.

The first time they questioned me it wasn't that bad. Mab slapped me a few times. Getting her own back, she was, for the pasting I'd given her in the woods. I said nowt anyway. And didn't cry out. Wouldn't give 'em the satisfaction.

After that, they left me alone in the dark for an hour or so. There were four mirrors in that cellar, one on each wall. Despite the dark, out of the corners of my eyes I kept glimpsing things. Witches spying on me. Making sure I wasn't trying to get away.

When Mab and her sisters came down the steps the second time, they meant business. Mab had my lock of hair.

Kept stroking it, she did, and muttering dark spells. Then the pains started. Pins and needles in my feet for starters. Next bad cramps in my stomach. But the worst thing of all was when I started to choke. It was just like cold invisible hands squeezing my throat. Couldn't breathe, could I? An hour of that and I told 'em everything they wanted to know. No hope of escape either. Even if I could have gotten free of the padlock and chain, they'd put a bind on me—a spell that meant I couldn't go more than fifty paces from that cellar. Hopeless, it was.

Told 'em about Tom and the Spook staying at Downham presbytery. Told 'em why we'd come to Pendle—to rescue Tom's family and get back his boxes.

"That's all I need, Alice Deane!" Mab gloated. "I'm off to Downham now to lure Tom back here. I'll tell him you asked me to bring him. He'll follow me for sure then. We'll have his bones before the night's over!"

I really hadn't wanted to do it. Last person in the world I'd hurt is Tom; I felt really bad giving his whereabouts away. Putting him in danger like that. And I was afraid that Mab's plan to lure Tom here might just work. She set off for Downham right away, taking her sisters with her.

After that it was all up with me. Said they were going to take both my bones and my blood just before dawn. Left me down in the cellar for a couple of hours, then some others from their clan took me out into the yard, where a big cauldron was bubbling, and made me sit on the ground nearby. Lots of other Mouldheels there—they all came across and gathered round me. Thought they were going to hit me, but they just stared down at me, their mouths thin, hard lines. Women and men, there were— not all witches, but every last one of 'em a clan member and sworn enemy of a Malkin or a Deane.

Someone shouted that the food was ready, so they left me alone then. But they didn't eat from the pot. Two big baskets full of roasted chicken were brought out, and they filled their plates and went and sat in small groups, leaving me be. Started laughing and chatting among themselves then. Nobody offered me any chicken but I was too scared and anxious to eat anyway.

An old woman was stirring the pot. She came across and sneered down at me. "Pain's coming your way, girl!" she gloated. "Lots and lots of pain. It hurts a lot when they take your bones. No matter how sharp the knife, it's still agony. Brewed you up a broth, though. I'll fetch you some now."

So saying, she went back to that bubbling pot and ladled some broth into a bowl. Came back and offered it to me. "Sip that, girl. Laced with special herbs, it is. It'll take away some of the pain — not all of it, but it might just make it bearable."

I shook my head. Maybe she meant it kindly but most likely not. Didn't like the smell wafting up from the bowl she was holding under my nose. Some believe that the more it hurts when they take your bones, the more powerful the dark magic, so it could have been a broth to make me hurt more. I couldn't take a chance. I shook my head a second time, and she shuffled away, grumbling and muttering under her breath.

Soon after that, Mab and her two sisters came down the hill. I was relieved that Tom wasn't with them. Mab looked angry, so something must have gone wrong. Went right up to the fire, Mab did, and spat into it. Flames died down right away. Then, on Mab's orders, one of the Mouldheel men picked me up and carried me back down to the cellar and left me alone.

I waited to die. Thought then of all I'd lost. I'd never see Tom Ward again. That hurt me most of all. Didn't seem fair. Tears came to my eyes, and I sobbed deep in my throat. I'd assumed that we'd have years together; that I'd be with him until he'd finished his apprenticeship with Old Gregory and then some more. Couldn't believe it was all over.

I was scared, too. Really scared. I thought of the knife, the pain, and dying in agony. It started to get really cold in that cellar. Witches kept glancing down at me from the mirrors on the walls. And then something else appeared in a mirror that was even more scary. I saw the ugliest of faces. Looked like a child, but it had no hair at all and a grown man's features with really sharp needlelike teeth. What was it? And then, suddenly, I knew. It had to be

Tibb, the creature that the Malkins and Deanes had made. It seemed to be looking straight at me, laughing and leering, till I turned away in fear and let a few tears come.

I heard boots coming down the steps and my heart began to race, my whole body trembling with fear. Then the door opened, and somebody was standing there holding a candle. But it wasn't a Mouldheel with a sharp knife.

It was Tom Ward. He'd come to rescue me. From a clan of witches, I am, and don't deserve to be Tom's friend. But I'd do anything for him. Anything at all. Even die for him if necessary.

Alice

Grimalkin's Tale

GRIMALKIN, the witch assassin, is deadly indeed and this plays an important role in the adventures of Tom Ward. The challenge is that she belongs to the dark, while Tom fights for the light. Their temporary alliances are frowned on by the Spook, who cannot tolerate any compromise with evil.

This is the story of how the young Grimalkin first decided to become a witch assassin; of how that seventeen-year-old girl challenged Kernolde the Strangler and fought her and her allies in the dark dell east of Pendle Hill.

· III ·

THE WITCH ASSASSIN

My name is Grimalkin, and I fear nobody. But my enemies fear me. With my scissors, I snip the flesh of the dead, the clan enemies that I have slain in combat. I cut out their thumb bones, which I wear around my neck as a warning to others. What else would I do? Without ruthlessness and savagery I could not survive even a week of the life I lead. I am the witch assassin of the Malkin clan.

Are you my enemy? Are you strong, with speed and agility? Have you had the training of a warrior? It matters not to me. Run now! Run fast into the forest! I'll give you a few moments' start. An hour if you wish. Because no matter how hard you run, you'll never be fast enough, and I'll catch and kill you before long.

All the prey that I hunt I will slay. If it is clothed in flesh, I will cut it. If it breathes, I will stop its breath. And your magic daunts me not, because I have magic of my own. And boggarts, ghosts, and ghasts are no greater threat to me than they are to a spook. For I have looked into the darkness—into the blackest darkness of all—and now I am no longer afraid.

My greatest enemy is the Fiend, the dark made flesh, to whom a witch must make obeisance. But there is one way that a witch can free herself from his fearsome majesty— one way to ensure that he keeps his distance. She need be close to him just once, then bear his child. After that, after he has inspected his offspring, he may not approach her again.

Most of the Fiend's children prove to be abhumans, evil creatures that will do the bidding of the dark. Others are born to be powerful witches. But a few—and it is rare indeed—are born perfect human children, untainted by evil. Mine was such a child, but I was not prepared for the Fiend's reaction. With a roar of anger he picked up my innocent baby boy, lifted him high, and smashed his fragile head against a rock. Then he vanished.

For a long time I was insane with grief. And then thoughts of revenge began to swirl within my head. Was it possible? Could I destroy the Fiend? Impossible or not, that became my goal. My only reason to continue to live. I was still young; just turned seventeen, although strong and tall for my age. I had chosen to bear the Fiend's child as a means to be free of him forever, and once I'd decided to pursue that course nothing could have stopped me. With the same dedication, I now sought the role of witch assassin as the first step to achieving revenge.

A scryer had placed the thought within my head. Her name was Martha Ribstalk, an incomer from the far north. At that time, before the rise of Mab, the young scryer of the Mouldheels, she was the foremost practitioner of that dark art. I visited her one hour after midnight as we had arranged. One hour after she had drunk the blood of an enemy and performed the necessary rituals.

"Do you accept my money?" I demanded.

She nodded, so I tossed three coins into the cauldron.

"Be seated!" she commanded sternly, pointing to the cold stone flags before the bubbling cauldron. The air was tainted with blood, and each breath that I took increased the metallic taste on the back of my tongue.

I obeyed, sitting cross-legged and gazing up at her through the steam. She had remained standing beyond the cauldron, so that her body would be higher than mine, a tactic often practiced by those who wish to dominate others. But I was not cowed and met her gaze calmly.

"What did you see?" I demanded. "What is my future?"

She did not speak for a long time. It pleased her to keep

me waiting. I think Ribstalk was annoyed because I had asked a question rather than waiting to be told the outcome of her scrying.

"You have chosen an enemy," she said at last. "The most powerful enemy any mortal could face. The outcome should be simple. The Fiend cannot approach you, but he can send many against you. He will await your death, then seize your soul and subject it to everlasting torments. But there is something else. Something that I cannot see clearly. An uncertainty. Another force that may intervene. For you, just a glimmer of hope."

She paused, stepped forward, and peered into the steam. Once again there was a long pause. "There is someone there. A child just born . . ."

"Who is this child?" I demanded.

"I cannot see him clearly. Someone hides him from my sight. But even with that intervention, only one highly skilled with weapons could hope to survive with the Fiend as her enemy. Only one with the speed and ruthlessness of a witch assassin. Only the greatest of all witch assassins, more deadly even than Kernolde, could do that. Nothing less will do. So what hope have you?" Ribstalk mocked.

Kernolde was then the assassin of the Malkins. A fearsome woman of great strength and speed who had slain twenty-seven challengers for her position. Three each year, as this was the tenth year of her reign.

I rose to my feet and smiled down at Ribstalk. "I will slay Kernolde and then take her place. I will become the witch assassin of the Malkins. The greatest of them all."

I turned and walked away, listening to the scryer cackling with mocking laughter behind me. But mine were not vain boasts. I believed that I could do it. I truly believed.

Three pretenders to the position of assassin were trained annually, but this year only two had come forward. No wonder, for most believed it was certain death to face Kernolde. The other two had been in training for six months. Thus half a year remained before the three days assigned for the challenges. I was given just that time to gain some of the skills necessary. Barely time for most to learn the rudiments of the assassin's trade.

But I walked out of that training school after less than a month. The other two trainees had no confidence, and death was already written on their foreheads. Grist Malkin, our mentor and trainer, had already prepared twenty-seven defeated challengers before us. What could he teach me but how to lose and how to die? And one more thing that I have not yet told you. Grist had trained my older sister, Wrekinda. She was Kernolde's fifth victim. One more reason to kill the assassin.

It was fortunate that I was a hunter and an able black-smith; fortunate that I was already skilled in the ways of the forest and crafting weapons. Fortunate, too, that as the third accepted for training, I'd be the last to face Kernolde. Even in defeat the other challengers might injure her or, at least, drain some of her strength.

So I trained myself. Worked hard. Invited danger. In a forest, far north beyond the boundaries of the County, I faced a pack of howling wolves. They circled me, moving ever closer, death glittering in their eyes. I held a throwing knife in each hand. The first wolf leaped for my throat. Leaped and died as my blade found its throat first. The second died, too. Next I drew my long blade, awaiting the third attack. With one powerful sweep I struck the animal's head from its body. Before the pack turned and fled my wrath, seven lay dead, their blood staining the white snow red.

I crafted the best blades of which I was capable. I wore them in sheathes about my body, which grew stronger and faster by the day. I ran up and down the steep slopes of Pendle to improve my stamina, readying myself for combat against Kernolde.

Did I say I hoped the other challengers would weaken the witch assassin? My hopes were short-lived. She slew each with ease; both were dead in less than an hour. On the third night, it was my turn.

The challenge always takes place north of the Devil's triangle, where the villages of the Malkins, Deanes, and Mouldheels are located. Kernolde chose Witch Dell as her killing ground, where witches are taken by their families after death. Taken there and buried among the trees to rise with the full moon, scratching their way back to the surface to feed upon small animals and unwary human intruders. Some of the dead witches are strong and can roam for miles, seeking their prey. Kernolde used these dead things as her allies, sometimes as her eyes, nose, and ears; other times as weapons. More than one challenger had been drained of blood by the dead before Kernolde took her thumb bones as proof of victory. But Kernolde often proved victorious without these allies. She was skilled with blades, ropes, traps, and pits full of spikes; once they were captured or incapacitated, she invariably strangled her opponents.

All this I knew before my challenge began. I had thought long and hard about it. In the shadow of the trees I stood outside the dell just before midnight, the appointed time for combat to begin. High to my left was the large brooding mass of Pendle Hill, its eastern slopes bathed in the light of the full moon that was high to the south. Within moments a beacon flared at the summit, sparks shooting upward into the air, signaling the witching hour had begun.

Immediately, I did what no other challenger had done before. Most crept into the dell nervous and fearful, in dread of what they faced. Some were braver but still entered cautiously. I was different. I announced my presence in a loud clear voice.

"I'm here, Kernolde! My name is Grimalkin, and I am your death!" I shouted loudly into the dell. "I'm coming for *you*, Kernolde! I'm coming for *you*! And nothing living or dead can stop me!"

It was not just bravado, although that played a part. It was a product of much thought and calculation. I knew that my shouts would bring the dead witches toward me, and that's what I wanted. Now I would know where they were.

You see, most dead witches are slow, and I could sprint beyond them. It was the powerful ones I had to beware of. One of them was named Gertrude the Grim because of her intimidating appearance, and she was both strong and relatively speedy for one who had been dead more than a century. She roamed far and wide beyond the dell, hunting for blood. But tonight she would be waiting within it, for she was Kernolde's closest accomplice, well rewarded for aiding each victory.

I waited about fifteen minutes. I'd already sniffed out Gertrude, the old one. She'd been close to the perimeter for some time but had chosen not to venture out into the open and had moved back deeper into the trees so that her slower sisters could threaten me first. I could hear the rustling of leaves and the occasional faint crack of a twig as they shuffled forward. They were slow, but I didn't underestimate them. Dead witches have great strength, and once they grip your flesh cannot be easily prized free. They begin to suck your blood until you weaken and can fight no more. Some would be on the ground, hiding within the dead leaves, ready to reach out and grasp at my ankles as I sped by.

I sprinted into the trees. I had sniffed out Kernolde. She was where I expected, waiting beneath the branches of the oldest oak in the dell. This was her tree, the one in which she stored her magic; her place of power.

A hand reached up toward me from the leaves. Without breaking my stride, I slipped a dagger from the scabbard on my left thigh and pinned the dead witch to the thick, gnarled root of a tree. I thrust the blade into the wrist rather than the palm, making it more difficult for her to tear herself free.

The next witch appeared from the left, her face lit by a shaft of moonlight. Saliva was dribbling down her chin and onto her tattered gown, covered in dark stains. She jabbered curses at me, eager for my blood. Instead she got my blade, which I plucked from my right shoulder sheath, hurling it toward her. The point took her in the throat, throwing her backward. I ran on even faster.

Four more times my blades cut dead flesh, and by now the other witches would be left behind; the slow and those maimed by my blades. But Kernolde and the powerful old one waited somewhere ahead. I wore eight sheathes in those days; each contained a blade. Now only two remained.

I leaped a hidden pit. Then a second. Although they were covered with leaves and mud, I knew they were there. For I had visited this dell many times during the previous months. I had gone there in daylight when the dead witches were dormant and Kernolde was out hunting prey in distant parts of the County. I had sniffed out every inch of the wood, knew every tree, the whereabouts of every pit and trap.

At last the old one barred my path. I came to a halt and awaited her attack. Let her come to me! Her tangled hair reached down to her knees. She was grim indeed, and well named! Maggots and beetles scuttled within that slimy curtain that obscured all of her face but one malevolent eye; that, and an elongated tooth that jutted upward over her top lip almost as far as her left nostril.

She ran toward me, kicking up leaves, her hands extended to rend my face or squeeze my throat. She was fast for a dead witch. Very fast. But not fast enough.

With my left hand, I drew the largest of my blades from its scabbard at my hip. This was not crafted for throwing;

it was more akin to a short sword with razor-sharp double edges. I leaped forward to meet her and cut Grim Gertrude's head clean from her shoulders. It bounced on a root and rolled away. I ran on, glancing back to see her searching among the pile of moldy leaves where it had come to rest.

Now for Kernolde. She was waiting beneath her tree; ropes hung from the branches, ready to bind and hang my body. She was rubbing her back against the bark, drawing strength for the fight. But I was not afraid, and she looked to me like an old bear ridding itself of fleas rather than the dreaded witch assassin feared by all. Running at full pelt directly toward her, I drew the last of my throwing knives and hurled it straight at her throat. End over end it spun, my aim fast and true, but she knocked it to one side with a disdainful flick of her wrist. Undaunted, I increased my pace and prepared to use the long blade. It was then that the ground opened beneath my feet, my heart lurched, and I fell into a hidden pit.

The moon was high, and as I fell I saw the sharp spikes

below, waiting to impale me. I twisted desperately, trying to reposition my body, but to avoid every spike was
impossible. All I could do was contort myself so that the
one spike I couldn't avoid was the one that would do me
the least damage.

The least, did I say? It hurt me enough. Damaged me
badly. The spike pierced my outer thigh. Down its length
I slid until I hit the ground hard and all the breath left
my body, the long blade flying from my hand to lie out of
reach.

I lay there trying to breathe and control the pain. The
spikes were sharp, thin, and very long—more than six
feet—so there was no way I could lift my leg and free it. I
cursed my folly. I had thought myself safe, but Kernolde
had dug another pit, probably the previous night. No
doubt she'd been aware of my forays into the dell and had
waited until the last moment to do so.

A witch assassin must constantly adapt and learn from
her own mistakes. Even as I lay there, facing my own
imminent death, I recognized my stupidity. I had been

too confident and had underestimated Kernolde. If I survived, I swore to temper my attitude with a smitch of caution. If . . .

Her broad moonface appeared above, and she looked down at me without uttering a word. Not for nothing did some call her Kernolde the Strangler. Once victorious, she sometimes hung her victims by their thumbs before slowly asphyxiating them. Not this time, though. She had seen what I had achieved already and would take no chances. I would die here.

She began to climb down into the pit. She would place her hands about my throat and squeeze the breath and life from my body. I was calm and ready to die if need be. But I had already thought of something. I had a slim chance of survival.

As she reached the bottom of the pit and began to weave toward me through the spikes, flexing her big, muscular hands, I prepared myself to cope with pain. Not that which she would inflict upon me; that which I chose myself.

My hands were strong, my arms and shoulders capable

of exerting extreme leverage. The spikes were thin but sturdy, flexible, not brittle. But I had to try. Seizing the one that pierced my leg, I began to bend it. Back and forth, back and forth I flexed and twisted the spike, each movement sending pain shooting down my leg and up into my body. But I gritted my teeth and worked the spike even harder until it finally yielded and broke, coming away in my hands.

Quickly I lifted my leg clear of the stump and knelt to face Kernolde, my blood running down to soak the earthen floor of the killing pit. In my hands I held the spike like a spear and pointed it toward her. Before her hands could reach my throat, I would pierce her heart.

But the witch assassin had drawn much of her stored magic from the tree, and now she halted and concentrated, beginning to hurl shards of darkness toward me. She tried dread first of all, that dark spell a witch uses to terrify her enemies, holding them in thrall to fear. Terror tried to claim me, and my teeth began to chitter-chatter like those of the dead on the Halloween sabbath. Her magic was strong, but not strong enough. I braced and shrugged aside her spell. Soon its effects receded, and it bothered me no more than the cold wind that blew down from the arctic ice when I slew the wolves and left their bodies on the snow.

Next she used the unquiet dead, the bone-bound, against me, hurling toward me the spirits she had trapped in limbo. They clung to my body, leaning hard against my arm to bring it downward so that it took all of my strength to keep my grip upon the spike. They were strong and fortified by dark magic, one being a strangler that gripped my throat so hard that Kernolde herself might have been squeezing it. The worst of these was an abhuman spirit, the ghost of one born of the Fiend and a witch. He darkened my eyes and thrust his long, cold fingers into my ears so that I thought my head was about to burst, but I fought back and cried out into the darkness and silence.

"I'm still here, Kernolde! Still to be reckoned with. I am Grimalkin, your doom!"

My eyes cleared, and the abhuman's fingers left my ears with a pop so that sound rushed back. The weight was gone from my arms, and I struggled to my feet, taking aim with the spike. She rushed at me then, that big ugly bear of a woman with strangler's hands. But my aim was true. I thrust the spear right into her heart, and she died at my feet, her blood soaking into the earth to mix with my own.

After taking what I needed, I lifted her body from the pit using her own ropes. Finally I hung her by her feet so that at dawn the birds could peck her bones clean. That done, I passed through the dell without incident, the dead witches keeping their distance. Grim Gertrude was on her hands and knees, still rooting through the moldy leaves, trying to find her head. Without eyes it would prove difficult.

When I emerged from the trees, the clan was waiting to greet me. I held up Kernolde's thumb bones and they bowed their heads in acknowledgement of what I'd done. Even Katrise, the head of the coven of thirteen, made obeisance. When they looked up I saw the new respect in their eyes; the fear, too. Now I would begin my quest to one day destroy my enemy, the Fiend.

My name is Grimalkin. I am the witch assassin of the Malkins, and I fear nobody.

Grimalkin

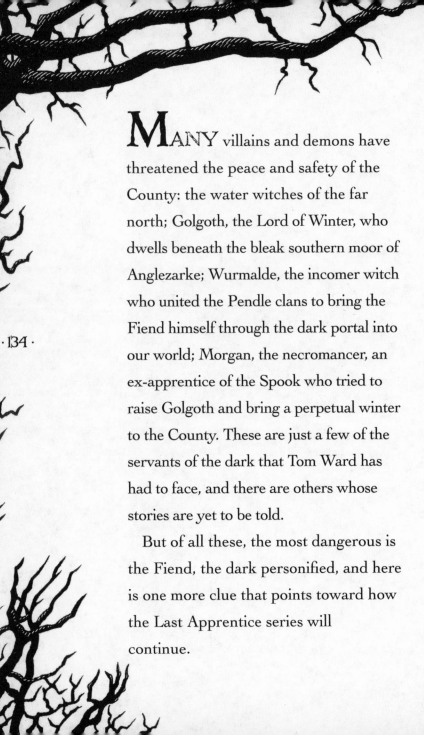

MANY villains and demons have threatened the peace and safety of the County: the water witches of the far north; Golgoth, the Lord of Winter, who dwells beneath the bleak southern moor of Anglezarke; Wurmalde, the incomer witch who united the Pendle clans to bring the Fiend himself through the dark portal into our world; Morgan, the necromancer, an ex-apprentice of the Spook who tried to raise Golgoth and bring a perpetual winter to the County. These are just a few of the servants of the dark that Tom Ward has had to face, and there are others whose stories are yet to be told.

But of all these, the most dangerous is the Fiend, the dark personified, and here is one more clue that points toward how the Last Apprentice series will continue.

The highest point in the County is
marked by mystery.

It is said that a man died there in a
great storm, while binding an evil that
threatened the whole world.

Then the ice came again and, when
it retreated, even the shapes of the hills
and the names of the towns in the valleys
were changed.

Now, at that highest point on the fells,
no trace remains of what was done so
long ago, but its name has endured.

They call it . . .

the Wardstone.

Does this hint at the death of Tom Ward
or maybe the Spook? And is that "evil"
the Fiend? Only time will tell. There are
many more stories to be told before the
answers are finally revealed.

The Gallery
of Villains

MOTHER MALKIN

Mother Malkin, one of the vilest witches imaginable, has been bound in a pit in the Spook's garden for years. Then the Spook's apprentice, Tom Ward, is tricked into giving her blood cakes, and she gains enough strength to break free.

She looked up at me then, lifting into the moonlight a face that was something out of a nightmare, a face that didn't belong to a living person. Oh, but she was alive all right. You could tell that by the noises she was making eating that rat.

But there was something else about her that terrified me so much that I almost fainted away on the spot. It was her eyes. They were like two hot coals burning inside their sockets, two red points of fire.

And then she spoke to me, her voice something between a whisper and a croak. It sounded like dry, dead leaves rustling together in a late autumn wind.

"It's a boy," she said. "I like boys. Come here, boy."

I didn't move, of course. I just stood there, rooted to the spot. I felt dizzy and light-headed.

She was still moving toward me and her eyes seemed to be growing larger. Not only her eyes; her whole body seemed to be swelling up. She was expanding into a vast cloud of darkness that within moments would darken my own eyes forever.

Without thinking, I lifted the Spook's staff. My hands and arms did it, not me.

"What's that, boy, a wand?" she croaked. Then she chuckled to herself and dropped the dead rat, lifting both her arms toward me.

It was me she wanted. She wanted my blood. In absolute terror, my body began to sway from side to side. I was like a sapling agitated by the first stirrings of a wind, the first storm wind of a dark winter that would never end.

I could have died then, on the bank of that river. There was nobody to help, and I felt powerless to help myself.

But suddenly it happened. . . .

The Spook's staff wasn't a wand, but there's more than one kind of magic. My arms conjured up something special, moving faster than I could even think.

They lifted the staff and swung it hard, catching the witch a terrible blow on the side of the head.

She gave a sort of grunt and fell sideways into the river. There was a big splash, and she went right under but came up very close to the bank, about five or six paces downstream. At first I thought that that was the end of her, but to my horror, her left arm came out of the water and grabbed a tussock of grass. Then the other arm reached for the bank, and she started to drag herself out of the water.

I knew I had to do something before it was too late. So,

using all my willpower, I forced myself to take a step toward her as she heaved more of her body up onto the bank.

When I got close enough, I did something that I can still remember vividly. I still have nightmares about it. But what choice did I have? It was her or me. Only one of us was going to survive.

(For the full story, read *The Last Apprentice: Revenge of the Witch*)

BONY LIZZIE and TUSK

Bony Lizzie, Mother Malkin's granddaughter, uses bone magic, and raised the young witch Alice, who becomes Tom's ally.

Tusk, Mother Malkin's son, is a monster of incredible strength. His name comes from the two yellow tusks that curve upward on either side of his nose. He lives with Bony Lizzie and obeys her without question, no matter how terrible a deed she asks of him.

There, standing at the summit of the slope ahead, was a tall figure dressed in black, carrying a long staff. It was the Spook, all right, but somehow he looked different. His hood was thrown back and his hair, lit by the rays of the rising sun, seemed to be streaming back from his head like orange tongues of flame.

Tusk gave a sort of roar and ran up the slope toward him, brandishing his blade, with Bony Lizzie close at his heels. They weren't bothered about us for the moment. They knew who their main enemy was. They could deal with us later.

By now Alice had come to a halt, too, so I took a couple of shaky steps to bring myself level with her. We both watched as Tusk made his final charge, lifting his curved blade and bellowing angrily as he ran.

The Spook had been standing as still as a statue, but then in response he took two big strides down the slope toward him and lifted his staff high. Aiming it like a spear, he drove it hard at Tusk's head. Just before it made contact with his forehead, there was a sort of click and a red flame appeared at the very tip. There was a heavy thud as it struck home. The curved knife went up in the air, and Tusk's body fell like a sack of potatoes. I knew he was dead even before he hit the ground.

Next the Spook cast his staff to one side and reached inside his cloak. When his left hand appeared again, it was clutching something that he cracked high in the air like a whip. It caught the sun, and I knew it was a silver chain.

Bony Lizzie turned and tried to run, but it was too late: The second time he cracked the chain, it was followed almost immediately by a thin, high, metallic sound. The chain began to fall, shaping itself into a spiral of fire to bind itself tightly around Bony Lizzie. She gave one great shriek of anguish, then fell to the ground.

(For the full story, read *The Last Apprentice: Revenge of the Witch*)

THE BANE

The Bane is an ancient, malevolent spirit—the only one of its kind—that is bound behind the Silver Gate in the catacombs beneath Priestown's cathedral.

The head of the Bane grew larger, the face becoming even more hideous, the chin lengthening and curving upward to meet the hooked nose. The dark cloud was boiling downward, forming flesh so that now a neck was visible and the beginnings of broad, powerful, muscular shoulders. But instead of skin, they were covered in rough green scales.

I knew what the Spook was waiting for. The moment the chest was clearly defined, he would strike straight for the heart within. Even as I watched, the boiling cloud descended farther to form the body as far down as the waist.

But I was mistaken! The Spook didn't use his blade. As if appearing from nowhere, the silver chain was in his left hand, and he raised his arm to hurl it at the Bane.

I'd seen him do it before. I'd watched him throw it at the witch, Bony Lizzie, so that it formed a perfect spiral and dropped upon her, binding her arms to her sides. She'd fallen to the ground and could do nothing but lie there snarling, the chain enclosing her body and tight against her teeth.

The same would have happened here, I'm sure of it, and it would have been the Bane's turn to lie there helplessly. But at the very moment when the Spook prepared to hurl the silver chain, Alice lurched to her feet and tore off her blindfold.

I know she didn't mean to do it, but somehow she got between the Spook and his target and spoiled his aim.

Instead of landing over the Bane's head, the silver chain fell against its shoulder. At its touch, the creature screamed out in agony and the chain fell to the floor.

But it wasn't over yet, and the Spook snatched up his staff. As he held it high, preparing to drive it into the Bane, there was a sudden click, and the retractable blade, made from an alloy containing silver, was now bared, glinting in the candlelight. The blade that I'd watched him sharpening at Heysham. I'd seen him use it once before, when he'd faced Tusk, the son of the old witch, Mother Malkin.

Now the Spook stabbed his staff hard and fast, straight at the Bane, aiming for its heart. It tried to twist away but was too late to avoid the thrust completely. The blade pierced its left shoulder, and it screamed out in agony. Alice backed away, a look of terror on her face, while the Spook pulled back his staff and readied it for a second thrust, his face grim and determined.

But suddenly, both candles were snuffed out, plunging the chamber and tunnel into darkness.

(For the full story, read *The Last Apprentice: Curse of the Bane*)

MORGAN

Morgan is a failed apprentice of the Spook's who has turned to the dark, using the creatures of the dark to make his own powers greater.

"The dead have had their lives. It's over for them. But we're still living and can use them. We can profit from them. I want what Gregory owes me. I want his house in Chipenden with that big library of books that contains so much knowledge. And then there's something else. Something even more important. Something that he's stolen from me. He has a grimoire, a book of spells and rituals, and you're going to help me get it back. In return, you can continue your apprenticeship, with me training you. And I'll teach you those things he's never even dreamed of. I'll put *real* power at your fingertips!"

"I don't want you training me," I snapped angrily. "I'm happy with things just the way they are!"

"What makes you think that you've any choice in the matter?" Morgan said, his voice suddenly cold and threatening. "I think it's time to show you just what I can do."

(For the full story, read *The Last Apprentice: Night of the Soul Stealer*)

MARCIA

Marcia, the sister of the Spook's love, is a feral lamia witch.

The floorboards were scattered with feathers, splattered with blood and littered with fragments of dead birds. It was as if a fox had got into a chicken coop. There were wings, legs, heads, and hundreds of feathers. Feathers falling through the air, swirling around my head, stirred by the chill breeze that was blowing through the skylight.

When I saw something much larger, I wasn't surprised. But the sight of it chilled me to the bone. Crouching in the corner, close to the writing desk, was the feral lamia, eyes closed, the top lids thick and heavy. Her body seemed smaller somehow, but her face looked far larger than the last time I'd glimpsed it. It was no longer gaunt but pale and bloated, the cheeks almost two pouches. As I watched, the mouth opened slightly and a trickle of blood ran down her chin and began to drip onto the floorboards. She licked her lips, opened her eyes, and looked up at me as if she had all the time in the world.

(For the full story, read *The Last Apprentice: Night of the Soul Stealer*)

Golgoth

Golgoth, Lord of Winter, is an elemental force, the most powerful of the old gods once worshipped in the County.

"Although trapped within the bounds of this circle, I can still reach you. Let me show you . . ."

Cold began to radiate out from the pentacle, the mosaic whitening with frost. A pattern of ice crystals was forming until I could feel the chill rising into my flesh from the floor, starting to numb me to the bone. I remembered Meg's warning when I left for home: *". . . wrap up warm against the cold. Frostbite can make your fingers fall off."*

The most severe cold was at my back, close to my hands where they were bound to the ring, and as the cold bit into my flesh, I imagined my frozen fingers with the blood no longer circulating, becoming blackened and brittle, ready to break off like dead twigs from a dying branch. I felt my mouth opening to scream, the cold air rasping within my throat. I thought of Mam. Now I would never see her again. But suddenly I fell away onto my side, away from the iron ring. I glanced back and saw that it was in pieces at the foot of the wall. Golgoth had frozen and fragmented it in order to free me. He'd done it so that I could do his bidding. He spoke to me again from the pentacle, but this time his voice seemed fainter.

"Dislodge the candle. Do it now, or I'll take more than your life. I'll snuff out your soul, too. . . ."

Those words sent a deeper chill into me than the cold that had shattered the iron ring. Morgan had been right. My very soul was at risk. But to save it, all I had to do was obey. My hands were still tied behind my back and had no feeling in them, but I could have stood, moved toward the nearest candle, and kicked it over. But I thought of those who would suffer because of what I'd done. The severe winter cold itself would kill the old and the young first. Babies would die in their cradles. But the threat would become even greater. Crops wouldn't grow, and there'd be no harvest next year. And for how many years after that? There'd be nothing to feed the livestock. Famine would result. Thousands would perish. And it would all be my fault.

(For the full story, read *The Last Apprentice: Night of the Soul Stealer*)

TIBB

Tibb is an inhuman creature created by the Malkin and Deane witch clans during a rare truce between them. He can see things at a distance, and can see into the future.

I could see nothing at all, but I could hear him—claws scratching and scrabbling, biting into wood. Then I realized that the sound was above, not below me. I looked upward just in time to see a dark shape moving across the ceiling like a spider, to halt directly above my bed. Unable to move anything but my head, I started to take deep breaths, trying to slow my heartbeat. To be afraid made the dark stronger. I had to get my fear under control.

I could see the outline of the four limbs and the body, but the head seemed far closer. I've always been able to see well in the dark, and my eyes were continuing to adjust until I could finally make some sense of what threatened from above.

Tibb had crawled across the wooden panels of the ceiling so that his hairy back and limbs were facing away from me. But his head was hanging down backward toward the bed, supported by a long, muscular neck, so that his eyes were below his mouth; and those eyes were glowing slightly in the dark and staring directly toward my own; the mouth was wide open, revealing the sharp needlelike teeth within.

Something dripped onto my forehead then. Something slightly sticky and warm. It seemed to fall from the creature's open mouth. Twice more drops fell—one onto the pillow beside my head, the next onto my shirtfront. Then

Tibb spoke, his voice rasping harshly in the darkness.

"I see your future clearly. Your life will be sad. Your master will be dead and you will be alone. It would be better if you had never been born."

(For the full story, read *The Last Apprentice: Attack of the Fiend*)

WURMALDE

Wurmalde comes from the same land as Tom's mother—in fact, they are old enemies, and Wurmalde carries her grudge onto Tom.

Mistress Wurmalde frowned, and anger flashed into her eyes. She took a step toward me: Her skirts rustled and the sound of her pointy shoes made two hard clicks on the cold flags of the kitchen. "Time to think is a luxury that you can ill afford," she told me. "Have you got an imagination, boy?"

I nodded. My mouth was too dry to speak.

"Then let me paint a picture for you. Imagine a grim dungeon, dark and dreary, crawling with vermin and rats. Imagine a bone pit, redolent of the tormented dead, its stench an affront to high heaven. No daylight reaches it from the upper ground, and just one small candle is allowed each day, a few hours of flickering yellow light to illuminate the horror of that place. Your brother Jack is bound to a pillar. He rants and raves; his eyes are wild, his face gaunt, his mind in hell. Some of it is our doing, but most of the blame must fall to you and yours. Yes, it is your fault that he suffers."

"How can it be *my* fault?" I asked angrily.

"Because you are your mother's son, and you have inherited the work that she has done. Both the work and the blame," said Mistress Wurmalde.

"What do *you* know of my mother?" I demanded, stung by her words.

"We are old enemies," she said, almost spitting the words out.

(For the full story, read *The Last Apprentice: Attack of the Fiend*)

GRIMALKIN

Grimalkin is the witch assassin of the Malkin clan. She is ruthless and unrelenting, delighting in torture and inflicting pain. The *snip-snip* of her scissors is a particular favorite, and she uses them to cut the flesh and bone of her victims.

Grimalkin might pull me back as I climbed over the fence. She could catch me crossing the pasture. Or the yard. Then

I would have to wait while I unlocked the door. I imagined my trembling fingers trying to insert the key into the lock as she ran up the stairs behind me. But would I even reach the fence? She was getting nearer now. Much nearer. I could hear her feet pounding down the slope toward me. Better to turn and fight, said a voice inside my head. Better to face her now than be cut down from behind. But what chance did I have against a trained and experienced assassin? What hope against the strength and speed of a witch whose talent was murder?

In my right hand I gripped the Spook's staff; in my left was my silver chain, coiled about my wrist, ready for throwing. I ran on, the blood moon flickering its baleful light through the leaf canopy to my left. I'd almost reached the edge of Hangman's Wood, but the witch assassin was very close now. I could hear the *pad-pad* of her feet and the *swish-swish* of her breath.

As I ran beyond the final tree, the farm fence directly ahead, the witch sprinted toward me from the right, a dagger in each hand, the long blades reflecting the moon's red light. I staggered to my left and cracked the chain to send it hurtling at her. But all my training proved useless. I was weary, terrified, and on the verge of despair. The chain fell harmlessly onto the grass. So, exhausted, I finally turned to face the witch.

It was over, and I knew it. All I had now was the Spook's staff, but I barely had the strength to lift it. My heart was hammering, my breath rasping, and the world seemed to spin around me.

(For the full story, read *The Last Apprentice: Attack of the Fiend*)

BLOODEYE

Bloodeye's true name is Morwena. She is the daughter of the Fiend, and the oldest and most powerful of the water witches. Some say she has been terrorizing the County for a thousand years.

Morwena surged into the air with the strength of a salmon leaping up a waterfall, her arms outstretched to tear at the Spook's face, though her left eye was still closed.

My master met her with equal speed. He spun, bringing

his staff in a rapid arc from left to right. It missed Morwena's throat by a hair's breadth, and with a terrible shriek of anger she flopped back into the water less than gracefully, creating a huge splash.

The Spook froze, looking down into the water. Then, with his right hand, he reached back and tugged his hood up, forward, and down so that it shielded his eyes. He must have seen the pinned eye and realized who he was dealing with. Without eye contact Morwena would not be able to use her bloodeye against him. Nonetheless he would be fighting "blind."

He waited, immobile, and I watched anxiously as the last ripple erased itself from the surface of the canal, which became as still as glass. Suddenly Morwena surged from the water again, this second attack even more sudden than the first, and then landed on the very edge of the wharf, her webbed feet slapping hard against the wooden boards. Her bloodeye was now open, its baleful red fire directed at the Spook. But without looking up, he stabbed toward her legs and she was forced to retreat.

Immediately she struck at him with her left hand, the

claws raking toward his shoulder, but he stepped away just in time. Then, as she moved the other way, he flicked his staff from his left to his right hand and jabbed toward her hard and fast. It was the same maneuver he'd made me practice against the dead tree in his garden—the one that had saved my life in the summer when I'd used it success- fully against Grimalkin.

He executed it perfectly, and the tip of his blade speared Morwena in the side. She let out a cry of anguish but leaped away quickly, somersaulting back into the water. The Spook waited a long time but she didn't attack again.

(For the full story, read *The Last Apprentice: Wrath of the Bloodeye*)

THE FIEND

The Fiend is the dark made flesh, the Devil himself.

I heard a noise from the shadows in the far corner of the room: a thump followed immediately by a sizzling, hissing sound. It was repeated twice more.

Suddenly I could smell burning. Wood smoke. The floor-boards. And then I saw that although time had stopped and everything within the room seemed to be frozen into immobility, one thing *was* moving. And what else could move but the Fiend himself?

I couldn't see him yet — he was invisible — but I could see his footprints advancing toward me. Each time one of his unseen feet made contact with the floorboards, it burned the shape of a cloven hoof into the wood, which glowed red before darkening with a spluttering hiss. Would he make himself visible? The thought was terrifying. I'd been told by Grimalkin that to inspire awe and force obeisance he'd appeared in his true majestic shape to the covens at Halloween. According to the Spook, some people believed his true form was so terrible that anyone who saw it would instantly drop dead. Was that just a scary bedtime tale or was it real? Would he do that to me now?

(For the full story, read *The Last Apprentice: Wrath of the Bloodeye*)